Langsmead Hall

Julia James

Pen Press

First published in Great Britain by Pen Press

All paper used in the printing of this book has been made from wood grown in managed, sustainable forests.

ISBN: 978-1-78003-680-9

Printed and bound in the UK
Pen Press is an imprint of
Indepenpress Publishing Limited
25 Eastern Place
Brighton
BN2 1GJ

A catalogue record of this book is available from the British Library

Cover design by Jacqueline Abromeit

To my children,
Simon, Liddy and Barney

With love and thanks for your support.

Chapter 1

"Houses have memories."

"Memories, Mom! Houses are made of bricks and mortar, haven't you heard?" said Toby.

"It's the occupants who leave their imprint. Every house has its secrets," said Alice.

Toby grunted. He was twenty-two years old and the subject of old houses and their occupants was of no consequence, particularly after being cramped in a small car for almost two hours.

"You have secrets, too. Don't you, Mom?"

"I don't, Toby. What are you talking about?"

"Then why don't you ever talk about your life over here?"

"But I've often talked about my childhood and what I did when I became an adult, haven't I?"

"Yeah. You worked as a PA and landed a job with a pop star. I know all that stuff. What you've never said is what happened after that, like when you met Dad. You've always evaded that subject like it's some place you don't want to go."

Alice reached out her hand and patted his knee. "You're probably right. I'm sorry, darling."

Toby shifted his position in the passenger seat and stared out in boredom at the passing landscape.

"Don't be so grumpy, Tobes. You didn't have to come."

Alice glanced at her Ivy League son, wondering, not for the first time, at how different her two boys were. Sport was Toby's great passion. At school he had shown a flair for creative writing but had chosen to follow a career in baseball. Joey, his younger brother by four years, also enjoyed sport, but his over-riding interest had always been the Arts. He was an accomplished artist and hoping to gain a place at the Slade School of Art. Alice believed he had the talent to succeed.

"Oh, come on Mom. You wanted me along. I know you well enough."

"Yes, you're right. I didn't want to come alone."

"Are you sure we're not lost? All these funny little roads are identical."

Alice glanced at the sign post and took a left turning. "No. We're almost there."

She drove through the village, excited by the familiar landmarks and then slowed down, her eyes peeled for the high stone wall that would signify the end of the journey. Her pulse started to race.

"Oh, look, those fir trees! Just a few more yards and we'll be there."

"Why are you so keen to see this old house again? You never said."

"Years ago I spent one summer there. It was the year before you were born."

Chapter 2

1987

Langsmead Hall stood in isolated splendour at the end of a sweeping gravel drive. Its wide, columned portico and tall, sash windows on the ground floor had the symmetrical features of the Georgian period, but higher up the building, the towers, turrets, pinnacles and gables owed more to the Neo-Gothic style so favoured in mid-Victorian England. Though the house lacked the classical proportions to give it the architectural merit of more auspicious manor houses, it was certainly imposing.

It was Alice's first visit to the house and she stopped her car in front of the heavy iron gates at the entrance to stare through the windscreen. Its eccentric appearance transfixed her. The June day was warm and sunny but when for a moment a dark cloud passed across the sun, the building was shrouded in a grey, eerie gloom that transformed it into the setting of some Gothic horror tale.

She put her foot down on the accelerator and drove slowly up the drive. To the left were tall pines growing along the perimeter of the high stone wall that enclosed the property and on her right a huge cedar stood sentinel, its great branches spread out across the expanse of green lawn.

The front of the house and the grand portico were deserted, and after parking the car she ventured round to the side of the property where she came upon a wide tiled veranda. One of the glass doors was ajar and as she was about to enter, she heard a voice calling her name. Perched on top of a ladder that was propped against the exterior wall was Ben.

He came down the ladder with a big grin on his face and Alice was amazed that this good-looking, self-assured young man was the same gangly youth she had known so well a decade ago. In the days when she had shared a flat with his older sister Kate, Ben had spent so much time sleeping on their sofa that he had become an intrinsic part of their lives.

"Really good to see you, Alice," he said, giving her a hug.

"Amazing place!" she said as Ben picked up her bag.

He ushered Alice through the French windows into a room of ballroom dimensions. An elaborate cornice offset the height of the ceiling, at the centre of which hung an enormous chandelier, its cascade of crystal droplets twinkling in the sunlight and casting shimmering patterns on the walls.

The flooring was deep golden parquet and as she walked across its gleaming blocks they conjured an image of the phantom dancers who had once tripped across them.

Kate had told Alice how hard Ben had worked on the renovations and when she commented on the beautiful floor, he nodded. "That was quite a challenge, I can tell you. It took a whole week of filling and sanding to restore it to its full glory."

4

Alice went across to the fireplace to admire the carving on the over-mantle.

"But whatever happened to the academic who got a first in philosophy?" she asked him.

Ben grinned. "It was money, what else?"

"You know, last time I saw you, you were working on those building sites," she said, recalling how Ben had taken on labouring work to get himself through university.

"And I remember how you both complained about my filthy overalls when I came back at night," he chuckled.

"No, Ben, it was the black rim you left around the bath that we objected to!" she said and turned to look at him. "I was amazed to hear you'd chosen the building trade as a career."

"Well, you see, Ali, after I got my degree I couldn't find a job and being stony broke as usual, I went to work for one of my former employers." He brushed a hand through his curly brown hair. "By chance I discovered an affinity with wood."

Alice raised her eyebrows. "Wood?"

"Wood is a very seductive material to work with, you know," he said with a grin. "I trained as a master carpenter and joiner."

Ben opened one of the double doors that led into the grand central hall, a magnificent square room with a wide central staircase in carved oak. "We should find Kate in the kitchen. Just follow me," he said.

After a brief tour of the downstairs rooms they walked along a passage towards the back of the house. Ben ran his hand along the golden oak panelling and murmured. "Feel the beauty of it. See how it lives and breathes."

He opened a door and stood back for Alice to enter. "I'll leave you to it!" he said with a wink.

Kate was seated at an over-sized pine table in the middle of an enormous kitchen. In front of her lay a pile of paperwork. She jumped up with a shriek. "Ali! You're here! You're early!"

Kate was wearing a sweatshirt and a pair of old jeans, and with her coppery hair pulled up into a ponytail, she looked little different to the girl Alice had first met when they were both eighteen. They had made friends while at secretarial college and subsequently shared a flat in Earl's Court. With her job Alice moved around a great deal and there was little opportunity to form new friendships but there was always Kate and she was her closest friend.

"It's been so long, Ali, almost six months," said Kate, giving Alice a big hug.

"You look terrific, Kate," said Alice.

"You too, Alice Ainsley," said Kate, holding her at arm's length. "Though you've lost a lot of weight, and as for that old jacket, I remember it from ten years back!"

"It was chilly when I left London," Alice said defensively and pulled off her well-worn leather jacket, revealing a linen trouser suit beneath.

Kate nodded in approval. "Well, that's better. Looks like you've finally started spending money on your wardrobe."

"Well I'm a lady of means now," said Alice with a grin. "The house is sold and there's money in the bank."

"You got a good price for it?"

"Yes, more than I expected. In fact, I should have enough to buy my next place with no mortgage at all."

She hung her jacket on the back of a chair and glanced around at the old oak beams and worn flagstone floor.

The kitchen was capacious enough to house a four-oven Aga, two large electric cookers, numerous oak-fronted cupboards and work surfaces, as well as two enormous Welsh dressers.

"Did Ben show you around?"

"Uh huh. I had a peek at the reception rooms. I think he wanted to show off all the beautiful woodwork."

"Who could have imagined that after all those years of study my little brother would end up a carpenter!"

"He looks happy."

"Oh, I'm not knocking it. His ambition's to have a furniture workshop and build his own designs. He's got the talent. So, what do you think of the place?"

"Looks like you've been busy!"

"I've been working my butt off, I can tell you." She cleared away the papers. "I was just settling up the last of the bills. Curtain makers, upholsterers, furniture restorers, there's no end to them. Now come and sit down and I'll open some wine."

Alice sat down at the table and smiled up at her. "Oh Kate, it really is fantastic. I'm seriously impressed. And with you running it, I predict that Langsmead Hall will be the finest country house hotel in the south, if not the whole of the country!"

Kate opened a bottle of Chablis and poured some into two glasses. She handed a glass to Alice.

"Well here's to you!" said Alice raising the glass.

"And congratulations to you for getting your life back, however overdue!"

Alice laughed. "It is a bit, isn't it? I'll be thirty-five in September!"

Kate grimaced. "Oh, don't talk about age. I've just found my first grey hair!"

She went across to the Aga, lifted a quiche from the oven and put in on the table.

"Help yourself to the salad," she said, gesturing to the bowl on the table.

She cut the quiche and handed a plate to Alice. "These last months have been nothing but solid grind, not to mention that major panic when the costs escalated and the auditors were breathing down my neck about not exceeding the budget. Remember when we last met and I wanted to chuck it all in?"

"That was just a lapse of confidence, something you aren't familiar with, Kate."

Kate chuckled. "Well, whatever, it was after your pep talk that I got Ben and his mates to take over, you know. They worked liked Trojans, got the job finished on schedule and only a fraction over-budget."

Alice took a mouthful of food. "Hmm, scrumptious pastry!"

"Yes, Maria does make good pastry."

"Your cook?"

"Yes. Maria and her husband Victor are from Malta. He's to be our maître d. I've put them up in the Gate House, that's the lodge by the entrance. You may have noticed it when you drove in."

The lodge's crenelated wooden frame was painted in bright blue and had reminded Alice of a house from a Nordic fairy tale. It was hard to miss.

Kate topped up their glasses. "Now tell me, how long can you stay?"

"I've only just arrived and already you're asking me when I'm leaving!"

"I'd ask you to stay the whole summer if I thought you would."

"That's not out of the question."

"Are you serious? What about your job? What about Humphrey?"

Alice had been working as PA to the pop star Ron Humphrey for the last five years and had been indispensable to his entourage. Polly, Ron's wife, was busy promoting her fashion business and had little time to spare on their three young offspring. It fell to Alice to arrange the school run and all the other activities in which they were involved. During the school holidays Ron liked to have the children around when he was touring. Usually they were accompanied by a series of nannies and Alice was responsible for their entertainment.

"I handed in my notice a month ago. I found Ron a replacement."

"Oh! Did you fall out or something?"

"No, nothing like that, in fact Ron offered me a huge pay rise to stay."

"You told me you'd dumped Richard and sold the house, but you didn't say you'd also chucked in the job. You really are making a clean breast of things!"

"Yes, that's the idea. The new owners are moving into the house today and my stuff has all gone into storage."

"So what are your plans?"

"None at the moment. I just want to take a nice long break."

Kate pushed away her plate and lit a cigarette. "Is Richard still on his spiritual journey?"

"I've no idea what he's up to."

"Now, that's good to hear!" She got up and spooned coffee into the cafetière. "You know me, Ali, I'd never jeopardise my life or career for any man."

Kate and Ben had been brought up by their mother and grandmother, two proud descendants of a founder member of the suffragette movement. They were strong, independent women and from an early age Kate had been imbued with their feminist ideals.

"So what finally brought things to a head?" asked Kate.

"It was that therapist, Priscilla."

"After the Sufi mystics and other oddballs he fraternised with, she sounded like good news, someone with her feet on the ground."

"Don't you believe it, she was the worst of the lot. What do you think of a therapist who relays the confidences of a client to his partner – and vice versa?"

"Combustible!"

"When I finally agreed to meet her, she described it as 'a highly proactive method of radical cognitive therapy'. Without further ado, she told me that I was interfering with Richard's journey of self-discovery. That, it seems, had come out of his lengthy and very expensive sessions with her. She was insinuating that, thanks to my dysfunctional childhood, I'm some kind of control freak."

Kate snorted. "Well, that's a joke!"

"And I was paying £90 an hour to be told that I was his jailer!"

"So, what was her agenda?"

"What do you think?"

"She wanted control herself?"

"Uh huh, and I willingly agreed to hand over the keys. It was just before Ron's US tour. Priscilla was the last straw and I told Richard it was over between us."

"So that was that?"

"No. He kept phoning to say it had all been a mistake until eventually I stopped taking his calls. When Ron's last venue got cancelled, I came back two days early and found them both in residence."

"What? Priscilla! She'd moved into your house!"

"It was early on Sunday morning and there she was with her two children having breakfast with Richard at the kitchen table. He said she'd been assaulted by her boyfriend and he'd offered them refuge."

Kate chuckled. "That bloke had the right idea!"

"Oh, I tell you Kate, I don't think I've ever been so angry. I sent the children into the garden and threatened him with the police if they weren't out within the hour. First thing on Monday morning, I put the house on the market."

"At the end of the day, don't you think this woman did you a favour?"

Alice grinned. "Yes. She did at that."

Kate started to talk about the hotel and Alice learned that the first guests would be arriving the following day.

"We've targeted the American market, the top end of course. We're offering a five-day break away in a glorious, traditional country house, you know the sort of thing."

"So every five days a new batch make an appearance, is that how it works?"

Kate held up her hands in mock horror. "Oh no, we're far too exclusive for that! What we've arranged is a two-day hiatus. The idea is that the staff will return to work refreshed and with renewed enthusiasm."

"That's a novel arrangement."

"A practical one," said Kate. "It means I can run a tight ship with a much smaller staff."

"Well, Kate, you put the Manville on the map and you'll undoubtedly do the same here," said Alice, recalling how hard Kate had worked to update a mediocre hotel in Piccadilly and turn it into a thriving concern.

"If I make a success of this, I hope to get a share of the action," said Kate.

Ben came into the room and took a beer from the fridge. She handed him a plate of food and glanced at her watch. "Julian will be along soon."

Ben pulled up a chair at the table. "Can you believe it? He's bringing his young nephew and niece to add to the mayhem."

"How young?" asked Alice.

"Ten and eight, something like that," said Kate. "They're the children of Felicity Shaw, the actress. She's Julian's sister in law."

Alice looked at her in surprise. Kate had never shown much interest in children. "Do you mean they'll be staying?"

"There wasn't much option. Felicity rang last week to say that the nanny had just walked out. She was in a bit of a state because she's leaving to go on a tour in Australia and there wasn't time to settle in a substitute," said Kate.

"What about the father?" Ben asked.

"Tim left her last year and he's living in Canada. Felicity got custody," said Kate.

"'Impresario Timothy Shaw leaves actress wife of twelve years for young Canadian actress.' Yes, I remember reading about it in the tabloids," said Alice. "But Kate, why here?"

Ben turned to her. "Because Madame Felicity is on the consortium that owns both hotels."

"Couldn't she cancel?" asked Alice.

"She didn't want to. Felicity has a lot riding on this tour, like getting back in the spotlight," said Kate.

"And it's in your interests to keep her sweet, eh, Kate?" said Ben.

"Hmm. Something like that." she nodded. "Look, Ben, could you fix up the curtain tracks in their bedroom, please?"

"Uh-huh. Do you want me to install that TV as well?"

"Yes, thanks for reminding me," said Kate. "There's the bedside lights, too. You'll find them and the curtains in the junk room."

"I could do that," said Alice.

"Thank you, Ali. It's all hands on the deck," said Kate, getting up. "And while you're up there, Ben, would you show Ali her room? I've put her in the green room in the east wing."

Ben led the way up the panelled staircase. He stopped for a moment on the galleried landing. "There are fifteen bedrooms on this floor, each with an individual colour scheme," he said.

Through an open doorway Alice glimpsed a large four-poster bed swathed in sumptuous blue and cream drapes and furnishings to complement. "Oh, what a lovely room!"

"Yes, Kate got in a designer. A lot of the furniture was bought with the house, though she picked up other pieces from auction rooms."

The room that had been allocated to Alice was decorated in shades of soft green that reflected the vista of the foliage outside the window. Ben opened the door to the en-suite bathroom. It had Edwardian furnishings.

"Your bathroom, complete with original thunderbox loo!"

Alice laughed. "Kate's always liked the authentic touch."

They climbed another flight of stairs and along a narrow corridor between the warren of rooms, once staff accommodation, and went into Kate's junk room.

Ben collected the curtains and Alice stayed behind to look for the lamps. She could find no trace of them amongst the assortment of fabrics and bric-a-brac and was about to abandon the search when she noticed a cupboard door set into the wall.

Behind the door there was a large area under the eaves that was filled with old books, boxes and artefacts. Tucked beneath the eaves was a cardboard box labelled 'lamps' and as she pulled it out, a thick layer of dust and cobwebs burst up in a cloud, exposing a small rosewood box hidden in the corner. She raised the lid and inside was an old doll, dressed in a faded muslin gown. She rubbed off the film of dust to reveal a porcelain face with a pink rosebud mouth and deep blue lifelike glass eyes. She stared at it for a moment, put it back in the box and carried it off with the lamps.

Later, on her way downstairs, Alice popped into the children's room. It was unusually large for an attic room, probably two knocked into one, but was so sparsely furnished that she decided to implement some changes. In a room on the other side of the corridor she discovered a small sofa and a table with a set of chairs and dragged them over into the children's room. After putting the beds to one end and hanging some floral prints on the walls, she gave it all a good dusting and stood back to assess her work. The room looked a great deal more inviting.

Chapter 3

Julian and the children had arrived and were sitting at the kitchen table playing a card game with Ben. Judging by the boy's expression, Alice's arrival was an irritating interruption.

Julian got up and took her hand in a firm grip. "Alice, it really is a pleasure to see you again," he said with a smile that reached his eyes.

Julian was a well-built man of over six feet. He had a self-assured manner and though not handsome in a conventional sense, his deep-set grey eyes and strong features had an arresting quality. Alice had only met him on one occasion and was pleasantly surprised by the warmth of his greeting.

She smiled back at him. "You, too."

"It's been almost a year if I'm not mistaken," he said, releasing her hand.

While she made a pot of tea, Alice recalled that brief meeting and observed him from across the room. She knew that he was a novelist and not one of Kate's usual circle. He was definitely not Kate's usual type. Kate was at the hub of the London social circuit and her list of contacts was extensive. Should an acquaintance want an introduction to someone of note Kate could arrange it.

Kate might relish this role, but it was hard to imagine Julian sharing her enthusiasm.

As Alice was reaching into the cupboard for the mugs Ben came up behind her. "We'd like to slip off for a quick game of billiards," he whispered, conspiratorially.

Alice glanced across at the children. "Okay. I'll keep an eye on them."

He gave her a peck on the cheek and disappeared with Julian.

"Hi, I'm Alice. And what are your names?" Alice asked, taking a seat at the table.

"I'm Tom. She's Poppy," the boy said. He had round blue eyes with a mop of blond curls like a Franciscan angel, though there was nothing seraphic about his surly expression.

Poppy was drawing a picture, her face hidden beneath long chestnut hair.

Alice picked up the pack of cards. "What were you playing, Tom?"

He shrugged.

"Okay, if that's how you want it." She put the cards back on the table and turned to him. "So, tell me Tom, what did you think of those old turrets up on the roof?"

Tom frowned and a voice piped up from behind the hair. "It was too dark to see much."

"Kate says the round tower still has stairs leading up to it. You can stand on the parapet and view the land for miles around," said Alice.

Tom looked interested. "Can we go up there?"

"No, not now. We'll have to wait for daylight."

He was pulling on a slither of wood that was coming away from the underside of the table. Alice told him to stop.

"What's it to you?" he said.

"I don't want you getting a splinter," said Alice, removing his hand.

"Who are you anyway?" he asked.

"I'm a friend of Kate's and like you, I'm a guest here," she said.

"We're only here 'cause Laura's gone away," said Poppy.

Alice turned to her. "And who's Laura?"

"She used to look after us," said Poppy. She looked up from the drawing and her hair fell back, revealing an eltin face. Her hazel eyes regarded Alice solemnly "Are you the new nanny?"

"Ah, there you are, Ali," said Kate, breezing into the room. "I've just had a late booking. It's one of my clients from the Manville and he's coming with his daughter. I can just about fit them in, though I'm afraid you'll have to move rooms tomorrow."

"Sure you don't want me to leave?" said Alice.

"Oh, no. You don't have to do that. Ben's going in the morning and you can have his room."

Alice nodded. "Would you like a cup of tea, Kate? I've just made some."

She shook her head and glanced at the children. "Ah I see you're making friends!"

She took out a bottle of wine from the fridge. She poured herself a glass and turned to the children. "You'll have your new friend Alice sleeping in the room opposite yours. That should be fun!"

"Big deal!" said Tom, rudely.

Kate opened her mouth to reprimand him but Alice shook her head. The prospect of a relative stranger as a neighbour could hardly be construed as fun. Kate shrugged and offered Alice a glass of wine. "I thought we'd all eat together in here tonight. Maria's made us one of her Maltese specialities."

Poppy looked up at Kate. "I don't eat meat."

"Well, that's okay then, it's a fish casserole," said Kate.

"She only eats fish fingers," said Tom.

Kate frowned at him. "Your mother said nothing about special diets."

"Then she expects them to eat the same as us, Kate." said Alice.

Kate looked appeased. "Yes, quite right."

Alice reached out to Poppy's picture. "May I take a peek?"

"In a minute, I haven't quite finished," she said, picking up an orange crayon and carefully applying it to the figure on the page. She put her head on one side to appraise it, then handed it over.

Julian and Ben had returned and Julian looked over Alice's shoulder at the flame-haired figure holding a glass in one hand and a cigarette in the other. He laughed. "Take a look at this, Kate. I think you've had your portrait painted!"

Ben came up behind him. "That's our Kate to a T! Well done, Poppy."

Ben was pinning the picture to the notice board when Maria and Victor came in. They were a middle-aged couple, both short and dark haired though in all other respects, they proved to be polar opposites.

"Victor's brother Joseph is the Manville's extremely efficient head waiter. You probably remember him, Ali," Kate said.

"Yes, of course I do," said Alice, shaking Victor's hand. "Your brother Joseph is unique, you know. He's as popular with the staff as he is with the guests."

Victor gave a shy nod and Maria's plump face lit up at the compliment. Maria was talkative and bubbly. Whilst serving the food she regaled them with stories about her brother-in-law as well as other members of the extended family, all of whom appeared to work in the hotel business.

Throughout the meal Julian had been solicitous of the children and even managed to bribe Poppy into eating the casserole. As Tom scraped up the remains of his dessert he asked Julian whether they could play cards again.

"I think it's rather late for that," said Kate.

Julian stood up. "We'll play tomorrow, Tom. Now it's time to get you two settled in." He turned to Kate. "So where are they sleeping?"

"But you said you'd show me that card trick," said Tom grumpily.

"Tomorrow," said Julian.

Tom scowled. "But you said..."

"Let me take them up," said Alice. "I've made a few adjustments to their room, Kate. I hope that's okay."

Kate looked at her as though she had turned into her guardian angel.

Upstairs in the bedroom Alice stared in amazement at the quantity of toys and games that came spilling out of bags and boxes.

Tom sat on the bed watching Alice unpack the last of them. "Oh, no, my Atari's not here. I told Julian I wanted to bring my games console. He's forgotten to pack it," he said.

"You could have done so yourself," said Alice.

"I packed all my own things," said Poppy with a small smug smile.

Tom glared at her. "Have I really got to share with her? I've got my own room at home."

Poppy started to arrange her soft toys on the sofa. "We've got a big playroom, too."

"Ah, but there's a huge garden here to explore," said Alice.

At the bottom of the bag was a hideous rubbery toy. Alice took it out and stared at it. "What on earth is this?"

"That's my Stretch Armstrong," said Tom, taking hold of the ugly green figure and demonstrating its malleability. "Julian says there's a lake here and I can go fishing."

"Julian isn't our father, you know," said Poppy.

"Mum says Dad's gone off with a floozy. She's really angry with him," said Tom.

Alice glanced from one child to the other considering whether a response was required when Poppy got up from the sofa. "I'm ready for my bath now," she said.

Alice put the last of the boxes into the cupboard and we went off to find the bathroom.

It had been a long day and Alice couldn't wait to climb into her luxurious bed. She fell asleep the moment her head hit the pillow, yet within what seemed like minutes, something disturbed her and she woke up with the uncomfortable sense of another presence in the room. She turned on the bedside light but there was nobody there. The clock read three o'clock and she turned off the light, but there was something hovering in the room. She lay wakeful in the bed, barely daring to breathe. It was impossible to gauge the length of time it lingered because each second felt like an hour.

She drifted off to sleep again. Next time she awoke sunlight was slanting in through the gap in the curtains.

She got out of bed and pulled on the curtain cord. Sunshine flooded into the room, dispelling any sense of the nocturnal visitor.

Chapter 4

Alice was late going downstairs. In the grand hall there was a small regiment of cleaners bustling cheerfully to and fro, brandishing mops and polishing cloths. Kate was busy, too. She was sitting at the kitchen table making floral arrangements, a mass of flowers and greenery spread out in front of her. At the other end Tom and Poppy were sitting in their pyjamas.

Alice poured herself a mug of coffee and sat down next to them. "Did you sleep well?" she asked them.

Poppy nodded and pushed away her bowl of cornflakes. "I only eat rice crispies."

"Yes, you've mentioned that before, Poppy. And I told you that I don't have any," Kate said, irritably.

Alice picked up the bowl of cereal and emptied it in the bin. "If you don't want this, you'll have to go without then," she said.

"But I'm hungry," Poppy said, indignantly.

She watched Alice buttering a slice of toast. "I'd like chocolate spread on mine."

Kate raised her eyes to the ceiling. "I told you before, we don't have chocolate spread."

Alice spread some jam on the toast and put it in front of the child. "It's jam or nothing."

While Poppy was eating the toast, Julian came into the room and announced that he was taking the children to the seaside.

"Can we get a fishing rod?" said Tom.

"That will depend upon your behaviour, Tom. I don't want any quarrelling in the car today. Now off you go and get dressed."

Poppy turned to Alice. "Alice, I want to wear my pink T-shirt, the one with the silver flowers on it!"

After the children left, Alice went up to the green bedroom to retrieve her belongings and carried them up to the attic. As she walked up the thinly carpeted stairs she heard someone following. The tread of the footsteps was light and she imagined it was Poppy returning to collect some item she had forgotten.

At the top of the staircase Alice turned around. "Poppy, is that you?"

There was no answer. The only sound was the creak of the floorboard under her feet. She waited a moment before taking her bag into the bedroom. After unpacking its contents, she took the doll into the bathroom to give it a good clean. She washed the cream muslin dress and hung it to dry on the towel rail.

When Alice returned to the kitchen Kate was discussing the menus with Maria and she was sent off to collect herbs from Dave, the gardener.

"You should find Dave in the back garden," said Kate, handing Alice a trug and a list. "Just tell him what we need."

The kitchen garden was situated behind a high brick wall and comprised a plot of land of about half an acre. It contained a prolific variety of vegetables planted out in orderly rows.

As Alice approached, Dave was digging up potatoes. He looked up and nodded.

"Hello," said Alice. "You must be Dave."

"Yes, that's me," he said, putting aside his fork. He was a big man in his late forties and had a friendly, weather-beaten face.

"My name is Alice Ainsley. I'm a friend of Kate's and I'm staying at the house," she said.

"Nice to meet you, Miss Alice," he said and rubbed his hand down his trousers before shaking hers.

He smiled with pride when she complimented him on the abundance of the produce and he told her that he had worked on the garden all of his adult life, as his father had before him.

"I came with the house, you see, Miss," he said with a grin. "Course, Dad still likes to come along and do a bit here and there. At one time he was head gardener here, you see, but that was in the days when the estate employed three full-time gardeners. Nowadays there's just me and a lad from the village as helps out."

Alice followed him across to the raised herb garden and watched him snipping large bunches of parsley, rosemary, thyme and basil.

"You must know the place better than anyone," she said.

He nodded. "Yes, I reckon so."

The mystery of that nocturnal visitor was preying on Alice's mind and she asked him whether he had ever heard that the house was haunted.

Dave placed a large bunch of parsley into the trug. "No, Miss. Can't say that I have as such." He paused for a moment. "Though it wouldn't surprise me."

"Oh?"

"Well, my gran always reckoned there'd be one troubled soul who wouldn't rest peacefully there."

"Who did she mean?"

"That was the young mistress, Eleanor Henshaw. She was the mother of them two children that drowned in the lake."

Alice stared at him in horror and was left momentarily speechless. She was going to question him further but heard Kate calling out to her. Maria needed the herbs.

"The boy's had no discipline. That's the problem, Maria…" Kate was saying as Alice went in.

Kate turned to Alice. "Tom was very rude to Maria this morning. She says she's never met such badly behaved children."

Maria mumbled something and nodded.

"Where do you want these?" Alice asked, holding out the trug.

Maria took the herbs and went off with them into the former scullery, now converted into a second kitchen.

Kate put the flower arrangements on the sideboard and went across to the sink to rinse her hands.

"Don't worry, Kate," said Alice, measuring coffee into the cafetière. "They're testing us out but they'll settle down."

Kate frowned. "I wish I had your optimism."

"I had enough practice with Ron's brood. Their mother was preoccupied with her own career and those kids were real little savages, but in the end they came round."

"I don't think I've got the patience."

Alice poured out the coffee and handed Kate a mug. "I found a rather lovely doll in the attic, a very old-fashioned doll actually. Is it yours?"

"No, not the kind of thing I collect," said Kate, taking a sip from her mug.

"It was put away in a box and looks as though it's been there some time."

"It probably came with one of the lots from the auction rooms. I got loads of stuff from them."

"Is it okay if I give it to Poppy?" asked Alice.

"Don't they prefer those dreadful plastic dolls they're always advertising on TV? She'd probably turn her nose up at it."

Alice sat down with her coffee. "It can't be easy for them, what with the nanny absconding and no parent around. That's a lot of change."

"Hmm, I thought kids were supposed to be resilient," said Kate. She lit a cigarette and sat back in her chair. "Well I had no idea how demanding they could be. How in the hell did Felicity expect us to entertain them? Julian's got a deadline so he can't be much help and the staff are up to their eyes..."

"Would you like me to take them off your hands?"

Kate's expression brightened. "You?"

Alice nodded. It seemed to her that she had already stepped into the role vacated by the errant nanny.

"My God, you're a star!"

A girl with bright blonde highlights popped her head around the door. "A van's just arrived with the wine delivery, Kate," she said. "Victor wants to know where you want it."

"Tell him to put it in the cellar, will you Suzie," Kate said.

"Right you are," said the girl with a smile.

"Who's that?" asked Alice.

"That's Suzie, a local girl," said Kate. "She wants to go into hotel management and I've taken her on a trial."

"She looks nice."

"Yes, Suzie's personable enough, though initially I did have to send her off to buy a whole new wardrobe. She arrived for her interview in a skirt that barely covered her bum."

Alice chuckled. "So when are the kids back?"

"I told Julian to keep them out as long as possible, poor man!"

"You know, you've never told me how you two met."

"Oh, that's rather a funny story. Felicity brought him over to the hotel for a drink. They'd just come from a launch party for his latest novel and I think she was showing him off, but she was so proprietary with him that it got up my nose. She's just his sister in law after all!"

"Where was her husband?"

"God knows! Anyway I decided to get better acquainted and a few weeks later I invited him to the hotel for dinner. He sounded surprised but he came. In the meantime, I'd done my homework and could talk about his books with a degree of intelligence. We seemed to hit it off and one thing led to another."

Alice laughed. "Kate, you're incorrigible!"

"Only problem is that one year on and I still don't know what makes him tick."

"He's good with the kids, particularly for a bachelor."

"He's been married twice, you know."

Alice was surprised. "What, two divorces?"

"No, his first wife was killed in a car crash. He got hitched again a few years later, but he's evasive about that marriage. Julian's what you might call a private person, though sometimes he can be downright secretive."

"What kind of novels does he write?"

"Detective stories and thrillers. He should have an insight. He worked for the Met once."

Kate was short-handed that afternoon, one of the waitresses having called in sick. Alice changed into a dress and helped to fill the gap. Tea was served from four o'clock onwards and by that time most of the guests had arrived. The first to appear were an American couple called Mr and Mrs Brewster accompanied by their daughter, Dallas, and her boyfriend Grant.

Alice accompanied them into the drawing room where Suzie was keeping vigil by the tea trolley. She was dressed in a white satin blouse with a black knee-length skirt. Apart from the silver-heeled stilettos, she looked a model of conservatism.

Mrs Brewster was very appreciative of the fine bone china and silver teapot that Suzie placed on their table. Alice heard Mrs Brewster tell her husband that all the best families took afternoon tea from Her Majesty Queen Elizabeth downwards who always takes hers in the company of her corgis at 4.30 sharp.

Alice learned that the family had been on a cultural tour of London and when his wife suggested visiting places of local interest Mr Brewster announced his intention to spend the next few days on a golf course. He asked Alice about the local golf club and she was relieved when Suzie intervened.

"We have the best in the county and we're well known internationally, too," she said, brightly. "The club is only ten minutes down the road."

She told Alice later that she had the information on good authority, having recently dated a pro at the club.

Alice bumped into Kate coming into the room with some new arrivals. "Do you know where Suzie is?" she whispered.

"She went to get some brochures for the Brewster party," said Alice.

"Couldn't it wait? We've got more teas to serve."

"Chill, Kate. She won't be long," said Alice. "She's showing initiative."

By early evening the atmosphere in the kitchen was fraught. Maria accused Damien, the assistant chef, of over-cooking the guinea fowl and when she told Kate that the dish should be taken off the menu, he flew into a rage and said she knew nothing about English game, or anything else for that matter. Maria retaliated by calling him an ignorant peasant, at which point Damien threatened to walk out.

Kate told Alice about the crisis when she called her into the office. Julian also appeared. He carried champagne and glasses.

Kate looked him over appraisingly as he opened the bottle. Julian was the sort of man who liked to dress casually and didn't spend a great deal of time on his wardrobe. This evening, however, he wore a well-cut charcoal grey suit with a natty pale pink waistcoat.

"Well, you have scrubbed up well!" said Kate, looking pleased.

He winked and handed her a glass of champagne.

"With the altercation in the kitchen, I'm going to need your support," said Kate. "Maria's in a strop and it's going to take my best diplomatic skills to diffuse the situation."

"So, what can we do?" asked Alice.

"I'd like you two to fill in for me in the drawing room. Chat to the guests and make them feel welcome," she said.

"I think we can do that, can't we Alice?"

"Good," said Kate.

She eyed Alice's blue silk dress. Alice had spotted the dress in Bloomingdales and though it was way over her usual price range, once she tried it on she was smitten. It had a flattering sweetheart neckline and fitted bodice above a floaty skirt.

"That's a stunning dress, Ali," said Kate. "Good to see you in something so elegant."

"I bought it on the trip to New York. It cost a small fortune," said Alice.

"I'm impressed!" Kate said with a grin. She smoothed down the skirt of her black two-piece. "Designer clothes don't come cheap"

Julian ran his eye over her outfit. "Is that why you raided that Oxfam shop again?"

Kate rolled her eyes.

"It's gorgeous, Kate," said Alice.

"It is very nice indeed, Katie, wherever you got it from," said Julian.

"Please don't call me Katie, Julian. You know I don't like it," said Kate. "And please make an effort with the guests."

He smiled roguishly. "I'll charm the socks off the punters, just you wait!"

It was close to midnight when the three of them retired to the sitting room for a nightcap. It was a comfortably furnished room that Kate had earmarked for her personal use. Kate pulled off her shoes and dropped onto the squashy sofa next to Julian.

He turned to her with a smile. "Well done, Kate. I'd say your opening night was a great success."

"Yes. I think you have some very satisfied customers, Kate," said Alice, settling into an armchair.

"Guests, Alice, if you don't mind!" said Kate.

"Oh, pardon me!" said Alice with a grin "Well I bet your guests have no idea how much work goes on behind the scenes – I certainly didn't."

"Well they are paying through the nose for it," said Julian. "I took a look at the prices in your brochure this evening."

"People will pay to be pampered," said Kate. "I quickly learned that our kind of clientele appreciate the personal touch, particularly our American visitors. At the Manville I used to keep brass nameplates for the rooms of our regulars."

"I don't see them queuing up here in the winter months, however much pampering they get," said Julian.

"It's a seasonal business, Julian," Kate said. "From autumn onwards the hotel is open for conventions, wedding receptions, that kind of thing. And next week I've got people coming from a TV company."

"Whatever for?" he asked.

"A major production. I understand they're looking at locations for a costume drama."

"That would be excellent publicity," said Alice.

Kate nodded. "Exactly."

"I trust you sorted out the fracas in the kitchen," said Julian.

"Yes. Eventually," said Kate. "Maria's feathers were pretty ruffled, I can tell you, but in the end I managed to persuade her to take Damien quietly under her wing."

Julian raised his eyebrows. "You did what?"

"I told her about his terribly deprived childhood and all the bad luck he's suffered. I had to lay it on with a shovel, but it worked. Suddenly Maria turned all mother hen and the look of bemusement on Damien's face almost finished me."

Alice laughed. "You've got the makings of a politician, Kate."

Kate nodded and smiled. She seemed to accept that as a compliment. "Well, you do need a lot of diplomacy in this business. It's all down to a happy and efficient staff."

"Don't Alice and I deserve some credit, too?" said Julian.

"Hmm, I saw you chatting up that young American girl," said Kate.

"It was rather fun," said Alice.

Julian glanced at her and chuckled. "Yes. You had that ageing American eating out of your hand."

"Who was that, Ali?" said Kate.

Alice thought of Art Sullivan's kind, intelligent face and engaging manner. She had very much enjoyed their conversation. "I think Julian is talking about one of your clients from the Manville, Kate."

"Oh, you must mean Art! He's the one with the late booking. Yes, he always stays at the Manville when he's on business in London. Art Sullivan is so low-key that you'd never believe he owns one of the biggest packaging companies in the world. He's got plants all over Europe as well as the US."

"So you keep a dossier on them all, do you Kate?" said Julian.

"Yes, it comes with the territory. And by the way, Art is only a few years older than you, Julian. He's also the father of that young friend of yours."

Julian grinned. "Ah, nice one! A rich Daddy, too. This gets better by the moment!"

Kate glanced at him sharply.

"Don't pay any attention, Kate," said Alice. "Art's daughter spent most of the evening with Dallas Brewster and her boyfriend."

Chapter 5

The next morning Alice was allocated the task of supervising the two students employed as chambermaids and the girls were carrying out their work so efficiently that she left them to get on and went outside to explore.

The well-manicured lawns were separated by colourful herbaceous borders full of early summer blooms. There were gravel paths, some lined with bushes of lavender and rosemary, and the one that she chose to walk along was canopied by a pergola of sweet-smelling roses. The path stopped at a gap in front of a high privet hedge and beyond it was a flight of stone steps that led down into a sunken, ornamental garden.

It was square and formal in design and enclosed by a weathered stone wall with bright blue aubretia spilling from every crevice. At its centre was a large lily pond with a fountain. The water sprayed from a gargoyle's head, its gentle patter harmonising with the hum of bees that hovered over the rock plants. On all four sides of this haven were stone seats set into the wall that offered the visitor a place to sit and contemplate. Like the old house, the garden had strong echoes of the past. Alice was reluctant to leave it, but she had to see the lake that Kate mentioned. "It used to belong to the estate and it's worth a visit," she had told her.

Behind the secret garden was a wood of tall silver birches, beeches and willows that cast heavy shadows over a dank pond. At the edge of the pond Alice noticed the remnants of an old stone bridge half submerged in the water. She surmised that a brook or river had once flowed beneath it and meandered across the gardens out to the fields.

It was such a cheerless, unwelcoming place that she moved on quickly and was surprised when, further along the embankment, just a hundred metres away, the still, dark pond opened up into a huge lake. The sun was shining down so brightly that it became a shimmering aquamarine pool.

Alice dropped down onto the grassy verge beside pink water lilies and dipped her toes in the water as dragonflies flitted across the surface, their jewel-coloured wings glittering in the sun. The atmosphere was so soporific that she lay back on the grass and fell into a doze, dreaming that the dragonflies were ethereal beings drawn back to earth by the magic of the lake. The laughter of children wafted across the lake to her and she opened her eyes expectantly, but there was not a soul in sight.

Later that afternoon Alice was up in her room, selecting an outfit to wear for the evening, when she heard a commotion on the galleried landing. She stood at the top of the staircase and stared down. Tom and Poppy were at the bottom of the stairs jostling to be first up. "Stop that racket at once!" she ordered.

Tom came crashing into her. "What do you think you're doing?" she said.

Poppy had followed him up the stairs and Tom pushed her hard against the wall. She let out a scream and clutched at her shoulder. "I hate him! I hate him!"

"Just stop this stupid behaviour!" Alice said, sternly. "You're staying in a hotel and there are guests in residence."

Poppy started to wail. "Well I hate this place, too. I want to go home. I want to go home now!"

Alice looked at the child's tear-stained face. "Oh dear, what a shame! That doll will have to go back in her box. She was so lovely, too."

Poppy's sniffed and looked up at her. "What doll?"

"Oh, just a doll I found," she said and turned back to Tom.

"Where is she, Alice? Please can I see her?" said Poppy.

"Go and look in your bedroom," said Alice.

Whilst talking to Poppy, Alice had kept a firm grip on Tom's arm and she now confronted him. "Why did you push your sister like that?"

"Because she's such a baby, that's why. She moaned about the sea being too rough and we ended up going round boring old shops. There wasn't even an arcade with machines to play on!"

"Well I went to the lake today and saw shoals of fish. It looks like a great place for fishing."

Tom visibly brightened. "Oh, cool! Can we go tomorrow? I can't wait to go fishing!"

"If you want me to take you, Tom, I'll need to see a marked improvement in your behaviour. No more fighting, do you hear?"

He nodded. "Okay."

Poppy stared at the refurbished doll with its freshly laundered muslin dress fanned across the bedspread.

Tom walked past and scoffed. "Huh! Only babies like dolls!"

Poppy ignored him and picked up the doll as tenderly as a mother with her newborn baby. "Please can I keep her, Alice?"

"So, you like her, do you?" said Alice, gratified that her efforts had not been in vain.

"Oh, yes, I love her. She's so beautiful!" said Poppy, stroking the doll's long dark brown hair which was now tied back with a red ribbon Alice had found in the junk room.

Alice smiled. "What about giving her a name?"

"Oh, I have. She's called Miranda."

Tom started to play with his Star Wars characters and Alice watched Luke Skywalker being armed with his light sabre in preparation for battle against Darth Vader.

"Just a moment, you two. I have something important to say so please pay attention," said Alice, perching on the arm of the sofa. "You must remember to use the back stairs at all times like Kate said. The main staircase is for guests only. And I don't want a repetition of what happened earlier. Is that clear?"

They looked at her solemnly and nodded.

Later, as she hurried down the attic stairs Alice bumped into Julian on the galleried landing.

"What's the rush?" he said.

"I'm late," she said.

"You're not a member of staff, are you?" he said. "Or is that something else I don't know about?"

"No, Julian. I doubt members of staff can spend half the day lying in the sunshine by a lake."

"You were there, were you?" he said. "Beautiful, isn't it?"

They walked together down the oak staircase. "Did you know that before the Reformation there was a thriving abbey where the house now stands?"

"No. That's interesting."

"The monks were a mainstay of the local community. They provided medical help for the poor as well as nourishment. That lake and its tributary were used to ferry their produce into the town."

"Until Henry VIII destroyed the monasteries," said Alice, recalling school history lessons.

"That was his brutal chancellor, Cromwell."

They had now reached the bottom of the staircase and paused for a moment. "Maybe Tom will be interested. I'll tell him about its history when we go to the lake tomorrow," said Alice.

Julian stopped and turned to her. "Ah, yes. Kate has told me that you have very kindly offered to look after them. That really is extremely good of you, Alice, though it does feel like an enormous imposition."

"No, not all. I wouldn't have offered if I hadn't wanted to."

"Well I'm very grateful. Kate, too, I'd imagine."

They walked across the hall's marble floor. "It may have escaped your mind, but the boss didn't insist we attend the cocktail hour," he said with a grin.

She put a hand on his arm. "Now that you're here, you may as well come in."

Mr Brewster was standing in the drawing room doorway. He smiled at Alice and moved aside to let them pass. "Your colleague was right, by the way. That golf club is top notch. I played eighteen holes today and it's a damned fine course."

She glanced at Julian. "You play golf, don't you?"

He looked at her, surprised. "I saw your clubs with the luggage," she whispered and turned to Mr Brewster. "Have you two met?"

He reached out his hand and pumped Julian's vigorously "The name's Vincent, good to meet you. My wife tells me you're Julian Askew, the novelist. She'd be real glad to meet you, too."

"Well, I expect you'll have plenty to talk about," said Alice, ignoring Julian's look of protest.

Across the room, she spotted Mrs Huntley and Miss Featherstone, two elderly English ladies whom she had welcomed to the hotel the previous afternoon.

She stopped by their table and gave them a friendly smile. "I hope you ladies have had a good day."

Miss Featherstone looked up at her. "Yes, very nice, thank you. We took a long walk around the grounds and discovered the sunken garden. It's a delight."

Mrs Huntley sat forward in her chair and nudged her companion with her walking stick. Alice heard her say something about the disturbing atmosphere in the house but didn't catch the rest.

Her companion shook her head. "It's not an appropriate moment, Charlotte."

"Is there something I can help you with?" asked Alice.

"It's nothing for you to be concerned with, my dear," said Miss Featherstone. She turned back to her companion.

Alice was curious to hear what Mrs Huntley had to say but with this polite dismissal she walked away. Passing by the Brewster party Alice saw Julian in their midst. He looked as though he'd been taken hostage and gave her a baleful glare.

Alice noticed that Erin Sullivan, Art's daughter, was sitting by herself in a quiet corner. She hadn't talked to her before and went over to introduce herself.

Erin had long black hair and deep blue eyes, an unusual combination that was inherited from her Native American lineage she told Alice. They talked until dinner time and Alice learned that Erin was on a sabbatical before starting her Master's degree in Fine Arts the following year.

"Is this your first visit to England?" asked Alice.

Erin nodded. "It is indeed. Dad often comes to Europe on business and this time Mom insisted he take me with him. She doesn't approve of my boyfriend, Steve, you see."

"And what brought you out here to the countryside?"

"It was while Dad was having meetings in London that I read a brochure about Langsmead and I told him how much I'd like to see rural England. When Dad discovered there was a golf course nearby he was fine with it."

"Yes. Evidently that golf course is a big pull for the men," said Alice, thinking how clever Kate was to include it in the brochure. She glanced across the room and noticed that Julian was still a captive of the Brewster party.

Erin was wearing an intricately woven shirt in a traditional Cherokee design and she was telling Alice how it had been made for her by a Cherokee friend when Art came to join them.

"Yes," he said, sitting down. "That friend of Erin's is a full-blooded Cherokee lady just like my grandma."

Art's fair complexion and sandy coloured hair bore no traces of his Indian ancestry. He must have noticed Alice's surprise because he looked at her with a smile.

"Interesting how genes can lie dormant and then pop up again a generation or two later."

Chapter 6

After finishing her household chores the next morning Alice slipped into the kitchen and joined Kate for a coffee.

"I hope you're okay with that room in the attic?" said Kate.

"Yes. I like it up there, despite the mysterious activity."

"Oh, God, are those kids playing up?"

Alice shook her head. "No, not them." She thought of her terror as she had lain in bed, her senses alert to an intrusive entity. "I just get the sense there is someone else keeping us company."

Kate frowned. "What on earth do you mean?"

"I think the house is haunted, Kate. In fact I'm certain of it."

"Oh, don't be ridiculous! You have too much imagination, Ali."

Kate picked up their mugs and carried them over to the sink. "By the way, I sent the kids out into the garden. I don't want them under the guests' feet."

"No, of course not. I'm taking them out," said Alice, going to the door.

"Thank you, Ali," said Kate. She chuckled, "And don't go filling their heads with your fanciful notions! There'll be a rational explanation for this ghost of yours."

Tom and Poppy were sitting on the front lawn.

"Alice, you said we were leaving an hour ago!" said Tom.

"Your watch must be gaining time!" said Alice.

On his wrist Tom wore a sophisticated digital watch and he liked to show off the many functions it could perform. He stared at it as though for the first time recognising its principle purpose.

Poppy glanced up at them. "Why doesn't Julian take us?"

"'Cause he's working on his bloody book, that's why!" said Tom.

Alice shot him a furious glare. "Do you want to go fishing or not? It's not too late for me to cancel."

Erin came out of the house and strolled up to them. "Hey, what are you guys up to?"

"We were planning to go down to the lake, Erin, but first I'm waiting for Tom to make an apology for his inappropriate language," said Alice.

Tom looked at her sheepishly. "Sorry, Alice."

Alice turned to Erin. "What are your plans today, Erin?"

"Oh, I just want to chill out. I spent all yesterday traipsing round a castle with Dallas and Grant," she said.

"Why not come with us?" said Alice.

"Sure, I'd like that."

There was a solitary figure at the far end of the lake and as they drew closer, Alice recognised Dave, the gardener. He was standing on the bank and steering a model boat across the water. Tom and Poppy watched with keen interest.

Dave turned to Alice and smiled shyly. "It's my hobby, you see, Miss. I've been building these boats since I was a youngster. This one here is modelled on the Bluebird."

"That was Donald Campbell's boat, wasn't it?" said Alice.

Erin nodded. "Yeah, he's the guy who broke the speed record."

"Oh, it's cool!" Tom said.

Dave navigated the boat back to the shore. He turned to Tom. "Want to try it, son?"

He handed over his remote control and Tom quickly got the hang of the steering and had the vessel skimming off across the lake.

Meanwhile, Erin was bent over another of Dave's boats. "This is real clever, Dave. There's so much detail. These paddles, for example, they're so tiny but so perfect!"

Erin appeared to have a wide knowledge of boats and Dave, getting down on his haunches beside her, described how he had modelled its features.

"Oh, what a cute guy," said Erin, dropping down onto the grass next to Alice.

The second vessel was now floating on the shallow water and they watched as Poppy, with Dave's assistance, propelled it out onto the lake.

"You'll never catch up with me!" Tom cried, watching the boat chug through the water.

"Of course, it won't, Tom. It's an American steamship!" Erin yelled out. She turned to Alice. "Sorry about that, but Tom should know the difference!"

"I expect he does," said Alice. "He just likes winding up his sister."

"I guess that's kids for you, and to think I always wanted a sibling!" said Erin. "You know, Alice, I thought Tom and Poppy were yours."

"No, I'm just taking care of them or doing my best to," said Alice. "Their parents split up recently."

"Oh, jeez. That's tough. Are your parents still together, Alice?"

Alice smiled ruefully. "My mother has had four husbands though I have my doubts that it was one of them who sired me."

Erin grinned. "What about siblings?"

"No, I was an only child like you."

"I don't think that's the best place to be. I want to have lots of kids!"

"Yes, I'd have liked that, too."

"Why talk in the past tense?"

Alice didn't want to be drawn on that subject and changed the topic. "Tell me about Steve."

Erin sighed. "Ah, yeah, Steve! He comes from the wrong side of the tracks as my Mom would say but she's such a terrible snob. She wants to split us up. What Mom insists on usually happens, like her getting custody of me."

"How old were you then?" Alice asked.

Erin nodded. "About eight. Then Mom marries this very preppy guy who works on Wall Street."

"And your father? Did he re-marry?"

"No chance! Not with me around for the vacations. I'm afraid to say I was a little horror. Whenever Dad had a new woman in tow I'd throw a tantrum or two and she was out!"

Alice laughed. "Oh, shame on you, Erin!"

"Yes. I guess poor old Dad gave up," said Erin with a grin. "Seriously though, I don't regret this trip for a minute. I've visited some interesting cities and learned a lot about his business. And coming here to Langsmead has been the icing on the cake!"

"So you aren't finding rural England too dull?"

Erin shook her head. "Oh, no. No, I love it here. I've taken a real fancy to this place, you see. There's something really special about Langsmead Hall. I felt it the moment we arrived. It's kind of spooky, the way these places are supposed to be, but there's something else I can't put my finger on. I just felt an immediate connection."

Alice was surprised and unexpectedly pleased to hear this young American girl echoing her own sentiments.

The next morning Alice arranged to take the children on a visit to the local swimming baths and as they were about to set off in her car, she suddenly realised she had forgotten the towels. On her way back into the house she bumped into Erin and returned to the car with an extra passenger.

As she drove into the municipal car park, Alice warned Erin that it was just a public pool and not what she was accustomed too.

Erin laughed. "We have them in the States, too, you know!"

The pool and its facilities turned out to be clean and well appointed. The visit was a unanimous success. Tom, in particular, was impressed by Erin's proficiency in the pool. He trod water in the shallow end watching in admiration as she swam up towards him with long effortless strokes, flipped over like a seal and disappeared back towards the deep end.

"I wish I could swim like you, Erin," he said to her later.

"It only takes practice, Tom," said Erin, swinging lithely up onto the concrete poolside. "When I was growing up, I spent all my summers by the sea and I practically lived in the water."

She dived back into the pool and encouraged Tom to swim beside her into the deep end. Alice took hold of Poppy's rubber support ring and they swam along behind them.

After lunch Tom was ready for more action. The lure of Dave's model boats was strong and once again they found themselves at the lakeside. However, that afternoon there was no sign of Dave. Tom's interest in fishing waned quickly and he started to taunt Poppy's solitary game with the doll.

"Hey, looks like Tom's got some buddies," said Erin, gesturing at the two boys who emerged from the woods and made a beeline for Tom.

The boys turned out to be brothers and lived in the village. Alex Johnson, the eldest, was Tom's age and Jamie about two years younger. The three boys went into a huddle and there was a great deal of giggling before Tom turned to ask whether he could go and play with them in the woods.

"Well, this is a turn up for the books," said Alice, watching the three of them scurry off.

Erin was very good company and both she and Alice were sorry when her visit came to an end. On the eve of her departure Art asked Alice to join them at their table for dinner. It was during the meal that Alice first learned about his holiday home in Florida. Erin told her they spent all their vacations there, glowing with enthusiasm as she described its location by the ocean.

"You'd love it, Alice," she said. "It's my favourite place in the world."

"Why don't you come over and visit us, Alice? We're taking a vacation there in the fall," said Art.

Erin grinned from ear to ear. "Oh, yes, Dad. That's a great idea."

The following morning when Art's limousine arrived on the driveway Alice took the children out to see them off. While the driver was stowing away the luggage in the boot and Erin extracted Tom from the back seat, Art took Alice to one side. "I meant what I said last night. We'd really like you to join us, Alice," he said. "Erin and I have both taken a shine to you and it would be so good to meet up again."

At that moment Erin came up and flung her arms around Alice. "You will come, won't you, Alice? You won't regret it, I promise you."

By midday the guests had departed and Kate pronounced their visit a success. That evening she invited Alice and Julian to share a bottle of champagne with her in the sitting room.

"No complaints, then, Kate?" asked Julian, taking a sip from his glass and walking across the room to an armchair.

"On the contrary. The reactions were extremely favourable. I couldn't have hoped for better," said Kate. She turned to Alice, who sat beside her on the sofa.

"You, Ali, were a real hit, you know."

"I was?" said Alice

Kate nodded and took a drink from her glass. "You remember Marion Brewster, the one with the red hair? She was full of compliments, telling me how nice it was to encounter such well-behaved English children!" said Kate.

Alice laughed. "You can't be serious!"

"Oh yes," said Kate with a grin. "She said they were a credit to you and your husband!"

Alice raised her eyebrows. "My husband?"

Kate gestured at Julian. He gave one of his roguish grins. "The Missus can take full credit for that!"

"Yes, she can indeed," said Kate. "Seriously though Ali, I wish I could keep you here. You're always so supportive."

Alice had a feeling that Julian wasn't coming up to scratch and that her comment was meant for him.

Alice may have laughed at Marion Brewster's myopic vision but had to admit to feeling some pride at the way the children were settling in and adapting so quickly to their new regime. Unlike Poppy, Tom needed outside stimulation and his meeting with the boys by the lake had been a Godsend and it was to be the start of a summer long friendship. Poppy was an unusually self-contained child, content either to potter about after Alice or to invent imaginative games for herself and Miranda to play. From that first introduction the doll never left her side.

While Alice was working for Ron she had become very fond of his wild young brood but sensed that her relationship with Tom and Poppy could develop into a deep attachment. The previous evening she was sitting on the sofa with Tom and listening to one of his discourses on the Star Wars saga when she ran her hand absently through his blond hair. Instead of brushing her away as might be expected he turned his head and flashed her such a beatific smile it would have melted the hardest of hearts. Alice thought about her reluctance to discuss the topic of children with Erin and realised how emotive that subject was for her still. She might have had a Tom of her own had life turned out differently.

That night when Alice went to bed the attic was silent but a few hours later she was awoken by the sound of someone crying. She assumed it was one of the children having a nightmare, but when she went into their room they were both sound asleep. Poppy had thrown off her bed clothes and as she bent over to cover her, the sight of the doll Miranda on the pillow beside her made Alice start. Even in the shadowy darkness the doll's features glowed with a lifelike intensity. It seemed to be watching her, its expression enigmatic.

There was no sound from Damien's bedroom and the door firmly closed, but as she turned there was a movement and a shadowed figure passed along the corridor. She ran back into her room, scrambled into bed and pulled the duvet over her head. It took a while to go back to sleep and when she did she dreamt that the doll had transformed itself into an animate object with human characteristics. Whether it was smiling at her with benevolence or hostility she couldn't tell.

Chapter 7

The following day Kate and Julian drove off to London and Alice was left in charge. The cleaners arrived early and were gone by midday. Apart from Damien, whose home was in Swansea and too expensive to travel to every week, the live-in staff had gone on their two-day break and they had the place to themselves. Damien's favourite possession was his guitar and he played it rather well. Tom and Poppy provided an enthusiastic audience when he took it out onto the terrace. Alice heard them demanding their favourite pop songs and Damien was willing to oblige.

Without the usual hustle and bustle and with time to herself Alice took the opportunity to wander around the empty rooms observing features that she hadn't noticed before. Although solitary she sensed that she was not alone.

She stood for a moment at the bottom of the stairwell looking up at the galleried landing, but when she put her hand on the knob of the newel post at the bottom of the banisters it felt like a block of ice. She pulled her hand away quickly and then something happened that rooted her to the spot.

Just an arm's length away stood a tall, elegant woman. Her heart-shaped face was framed by corn coloured hair that escaped in tendrils from a dove-grey pillbox hat arranged on her head at a jaunty angle. With it she wore a long-fitted coat bordered in grey fox.

She turned and looked up the staircase as she pulled off her long kid gloves. "George! Emily! Where are you?"

The next moment a boy and a girl appeared on the landing above.

"Mama, Mama! You're back!" the girl cried, excitedly. A doll dangled from her hand. It was the doll from the attic.

The children ran down the stairs and the woman opened her arms. A girl dressed in a starched white cap and apron followed down the staircase.

With her arms wrapped around the children, the woman looked up at her. "Good afternoon, Janet. I trust you are well."

The girl made a bob, "Yes, Ma'am. I'm very well."

"I hope my babies have been behaving themselves," said the mother.

"Yes, Ma'am," Janet said with a nod.

"We were just going to the lake, Mama. It's all frozen over," said the boy.

"It's been frozen three days now and the master says it's solid enough to walk on, Ma'am," said Janet.

"Oh, is the master home?" the woman asked.

"Yes, ma'am, he's been here these last two days."

"Will you come with us, Mama?" said the boy.

The girl pulled on her mother's hand. "Oh, yes, please come, Mama."

"I'll have to change out of these clothes and see your Papa first, but I'll try and join you later. In the meantime, take care on the ice and do exactly as Janet says. Promise me?"

The woman smiled fondly at their departing figures and turned to go up the stairs. The stern tones of a male voice arrested her progress.

"I see you've decided to come home, Eleanor," he said.

It was Henry, her husband, a portly middle-aged man with receding dark hair streaked with silver and a carefully trimmed moustache above a thin upper lip.

She turned around to face him. "Oh Henry, you startled me."

"We were expecting you back first thing this morning, Eleanor," he said, his tone admonishing.

"Yes, Henry. I'm afraid I had to take a later train," she said.

"You should have informed me," he said. "It may have escaped your memory, but I have had a telephone installed. The purpose of having a telephone is to convey such information."

"I'm sorry, Henry. I didn't realise you'd be here."

"Mary will be serving tea in the library in ten minutes. I should like you to join me," he said.

Henry was a man accustomed to obedience. He turned on his heel and walked away. Eleanor watched him go and frowned.

Henry was the senior partner of the law firm that had handled Eleanor's family's legal affairs. It was after the sudden death of her father Patrick from a heart attack at the age of fifty-four that Eleanor first came into contact with Henry. It was from him that Eleanor and her mother Melanie learned that Patrick's estate had been put in jeopardy by a fraudulent business associate.

A week after her father's death Eleanor and her mother had been summoned to Henry's chambers where he informed them of the dire financial straits in which they were left. "I'm afraid Mr Gilmore took bad advice and was persuaded to invest all his capital in a bogus business," Henry told them.

Her mother stared at him with blank eyes. Eleanor took one look at her and suggested they should go outside for some air. Henry was most solicitous. He accompanied them out to the street and instructed one of his clerks to fetch a hansom cab to take Eleanor's mother home.

"I'm afraid my mother is not in the best of health. It's the shock of my father's death," said Eleanor, sitting down once more in Henry's office. A young clerk came into the room with a tray of refreshments.

Eleanor sipped at her cordial while Henry studied the file of papers on his desk. After a few minutes he looked up at Eleanor and cleared his throat.

"These investments I mentioned took place over a period of five years and I see here that there is also a loan borrowed against the family home," he said solemnly.

For the first time in her life Eleanor felt fury at her father but it passed in a moment. During the last year the carefree, generous father she knew had changed into an anxious, troubled man. She had watched him as he pored over the household accounts with a worried frown and was surprised when one day she overheard him question her mother about what she was spending on clothes. Her mother had laughed it off, telling Eleanor that her father was turning into an old Scrooge, but Eleanor realised that he would not have tried to check this expense without good reason.

Eleanor resembled her father both in looks and temperament and they had always shared a strong bond. Having guessed the nature of his concern she tactfully suggested ways of making economies, but her father was a proud man and his response was to pat her hand or stoke her cheek and tell her that he didn't want her concerned with such things.

"This is very hard to understand, Mr Henshaw. My father was not a reckless man," said Eleanor.

"I'm afraid your father is not alone. I have seen lesser men than he be duped by a fraudulent investment scheme. The people who operate them have great cunning and can be very persuasive."

"And my father didn't consult you before putting his trust in these people?"

"Regrettably not, Miss Gilmore. I would have looked into their credentials."

"Is there nothing we can do?"

"I am currently chasing up these creditors and we have a strong case against them. They have had no access to the deeds of the house. The deeds are lodged with us which makes their claims invalid."

"Thank God for that. At least we will still have our equity in the house."

He looked up at her and nodded, impressed by her quiet grasp of the situation.

"We are in the process of investigating the legalities of these transactions and attempting to make contact with a Mr Lewisham, your father's business associate. It is imperative that we find Mr Lewisham in order to clarify certain irregularities that could be beneficial to your case."

"So there is hope we may recoup some of these losses?"

"I would not depend upon it. From my enquiries to date, it would appear that this gentleman is of a dubious reputation."

"Do you hold out much hope, Mr Henshaw?"

"I should prefer not to say at this stage, Miss Gilmore, but let me assure you that I will be doing my very best on your behalf."

On a damp November morning five months later Henry paid an unexpected visit to the family home in Hammersmith. Since their first meeting he had kept in regular contact and Eleanor had been summoned twice more to his office. On the second occasion Henry informed her that Mr Lewisham had embezzled the funds from her father's estate and gone to ground. Henry had also made appointments to call at the house though these visits appeared to be prompted by courtesy because there was still no further information concerning Mr Lewisham.

As each day passed with no news of Mr Lewisham's whereabouts Eleanor was forced to accept the grim reality of their situation. She took charge of the household's day-to-day living costs, eking out the remnants of her mother's family legacy and started negotiations regarding the sale of their property. She dreaded the moment of telling her mother that their departure from the house could no longer be delayed and hadn't yet mentioned her aunt and uncle's generous offer of shelter in their home, knowing that her mother would be mortified to have to accept their charity.

When Eleanor first broached the subject of the house sale her mother burst into tears and was inconsolable. Afterwards she was unwilling to discuss the matter further. The family doctor had prescribed laudanum for her nerves and Eleanor was increasingly worried about her mother's need for the drug.

The drawing room of the Queen Anne house was situated on the first floor and Eleanor was standing at the window looking out at the river when Rose, their last remaining servant, announced Henry's arrival. It was a view that Eleanor had grown up with, though never taken for granted, particularly now when the privileged life she had lived in that house was to end. Her interview for the position of typist in the local town hall would come as a shock to her mother who knew nothing of Eleanor's clandestine outings to attend evening classes.

The only person in whom she confided was Declan, the man she was in love with. She also told Declan of her disappointment at the meagre salary they were offering. "So much for my efforts to become the bread winner!" she had smiled, ruefully.

It was almost a year since their first meeting which took place at a party held by her aunt and uncle to celebrate her eighteenth birthday in September 1904. It was an occasion that Eleanor would never forget. Declan had been invited as a friend of Jonathan. He and Eleanor were instantly attracted and soon fell in love. Declan was an impoverished medical student and although they wished to do so, there was no question of formalising their relationship until he had completed his medical studies.

"Your efforts have not been in vain, my love," he had said to her, fondly. "Once I have my country practice we can make good use of your office skills."

She looked up at his handsome smiling face in surprise. "A country doctor! What are you talking about? You plan to be a surgeon just like your father."

"But that would mean more studying and even longer to wait before we can be married," he said.

Everything had changed after the death of her father, even Declan's career ambitions, Eleanor thought bitterly. The last time she met him they had walked together in Richmond Park. He had talked with such enthusiasm about their future together that Eleanor couldn't help smiling, however far off that day might be.

Henry's unsolicited visit might well be prompted by good news and Eleanor considered asking her mother to join them but decided against it. Melanie was suffering from one of her frequent migraines and was lying in her darkened bedroom, her eyes shrouded beneath a black cloth.

Eleanor turned to their maid with hope in her heart. "Please ask Mr Henshaw to come in, Rose."

Eleanor walked towards him and extended her hand. "Mr Henshaw, how good of you to come."

He took her hand with a small brief nod of his head. "I'm glad to find you at home, Miss Gilmore."

"Do be seated," she said, directing him to a wing chair. "I'm afraid my mother is indisposed today."

"I'm sorry to hear that," he said, sitting down. "But it is in fact you that I have come to see."

"Perhaps you would care for some sherry, Mr Henshaw?" said Eleanor, taking a seat opposite him.

"Yes, thank you," he said, adjusting the stiff cuffs of his shirt with the fastidious precision he applied to all his actions.

Rose hovered in the doorway. She was a kindly, simple woman of about fifty and had been in service with Melanie's family for longer than she or anyone else could remember. Eleanor nodded to Rose. She bustled off to bring the sherry.

Eleanor turned to Henry. "So, Mr Henshaw, do you have any news for us?"

"Yes. I'm afraid the news is that Lewisham has absconded to South America. The embezzled funds have been deposited in Bolivia where he appears to have an interest in a tin mining company. The man is a complete scoundrel."

Eleanor felt crushed. "Surely there is something we can do? Won't he be arrested?"

"Too late. We have no jurisdiction over the Bolivian authorities."

"So all is lost! Oh, my God!"

"I am all too aware of what you have suffered, Miss Gilmore."

"To speak frankly, Mr Henshaw, the effect of leaving this house on my mother is my major concern."

He was silent for a moment, regarding her thoughtfully, his fingers pressed together into a pyramid. "That doesn't necessarily have to be the case."

Eleanor frowned. "But we are no longer in a position to maintain the property."

Rosie returned to the room with a silver tray laden with a sherry decanter, glasses and a plate of biscuits.

"Well, I have been doing some thinking," he said after Rosie left the room. "May I call you Eleanor?"

Eleanor nodded. "Of course."

"You see, Eleanor, I am approaching forty and it is time I was married."

Eleanor's thoughts flew to her mother. Melanie must be only two or three years Henry's senior and she had retained her small, slender figure and pretty features. Eleanor had noticed how the males of their acquaintance responded to her charms and she believed that Melanie could soon have this rather serious man eating out of her hand just as she had done with Patrick. After all was said and done Mr Henshaw's time and efforts on their behalf went way beyond the call of duty. No one could ever replace her father, but should Melanie be agreeable there could be many advantages to such a match.

He cleared his throat. "I have watched the way you have conducted yourself over the last months and it is much to your credit, Eleanor. You are clearly a very sensible young woman."

"Well, thank you, Mr Henshaw. You have been a good friend to us."

He took a sip from his sherry glass. "And I should like to be more than that."

Eleanor nodded.

"I know how you like plain speech, Eleanor, so I won't beat about the bush. I should like you to become my wife."

Eleanor stared at him aghast. For a moment she lost her grasp on the sherry glass and some spilt onto the skirt of her dress.

"I will ensure that your mother can live in the manner to which she is accustomed. Have no worries there."

Eleanor knew that a response was required from her, but she could think only of Declan. "Excuse me a moment," she said in a whisper. She got up and walked across to the window to compose herself. Through the mist that had settled over the river a steamboat appeared. She watched it chugging through the water and past the house. How she wished she could climb aboard and let it take her wherever it was going. It didn't matter where.

"I will give you a week to consider my proposal, Eleanor," she heard the voice behind her say.

There was no talk of love or affection. He was offering an arrangement that would save her father's reputation and provide a future for her mother.

"You say you will take care of my mother?" she said quietly.

"Yes, Eleanor. Your mother may remain in this house for as long as she wishes and I will ensure that she receives an annuity."

"That's very generous, Mr Henshaw," she said.

He got up and came to stand beside her. "Should you decide to accept my offer, you may be sure that I will fulfil my side of the agreement. I am not a man to go back on his word," he said.

Eleanor turned around. Their faces were at the same level and she stared into his unfathomable dark eyes. "I am honoured by your proposal, Mr Henshaw. I will give it my consideration."

"Henry, please."

"Very well, Henry."

"I shall return in one week's time for your answer, Eleanor."

Chapter 8

Eleanor announced her betrothal to her relatives the day after she accepted Henry's proposal. It had been a tortuously long week during which she wrestled between heart and head; love and duty. At night she tossed and turned, only sleeping in snatches and there were dark shadows beneath her eyes. It wasn't until the sixth day that a decision was arrived at.

Eleanor was eating breakfast in the kitchen when Rose came into the room.

"Your Mama has refused her breakfast, nor did she eat her supper last night. I fear she is sickening for something," she said, looking worried.

Eleanor sat down on the bed and took her mother's small dainty hand in her own. "Mama, what's the matter?"

"I'm unwell, child," she said in a whisper.

"But the doctor saw you only last week and he said there was nothing wrong with you physically."

"He doesn't understand."

"Understand what, Mama?"

"Tell me what there is left to live for?"

"You have everything to live for, Mama. You're just feeling low at the moment."

"And don't I have reason? How can I countenance the idea of living in a poky little house with no servants. It's not what I'm used to."

"But Mama, we have discussed this before. You have me and you have Rose."

"Rose! She doesn't know how to wait at table and as for her cooking, it's atrocious."

Eleanor sighed. "Oh, Mama!"

Melanie pulled away her hand and closed her eyes. "How can I ever hold my head up again?"

Eleanor looked at her mother in despair. "You will."

She got up and started to pace the room. "I think you should know, Mama. Mr Henshaw has asked me to marry him."

Melanie's eyes flew open. "Mr Henshaw! Oh, Eleanor, how wonderful! But when did this take place?"

"Almost a week ago."

Melanie sat up in bed. "Why didn't you tell me before?"

"Because I've been considering his proposal."

"What is there to consider, Eleanor? Mr Henshaw will take care of us. He will reverse our fortune. Mr Henshaw will be our saviour!"

"Hmm. A knight in shining armour," Eleanor muttered, bitterly.

Melanie swung her legs out of the bed and reached for her dressing gown. "Oh, my child, this is such splendid news. Mr Henshaw is a very honourable man. You are a fortunate young woman indeed. Your dear Papa would be so proud of you."

She went to her dressing table and sat down. "I must send a note to Mr Henshaw directly. We will get Rose to collect Papa's finest wine from the cellar to celebrate your engagement. Oh, there is so much to be done!" She turned to Eleanor. "Be a good girl and go and find Rose. Tell her to bring up my breakfast tray immediately. Suddenly I have such an appetite."

Two days later Eleanor visited her aunt and uncle to inform them of her engagement. She was taking tea with her relatives in their parlour when she made her announcement.

Her uncle, Arthur Farthingale, was the first to react. He was married to Melanie's elder sister Joan and was eternally grateful that he had chosen her to be his wife. When the sisters were young, it was the flighty Melanie that the young men sought out. Joan was a serious girl and lacked her sister's prettiness and vivacity, but it was the intelligence that shone from her bright brown eyes and her sweet disposition that had first attracted him.

Arthur set down his tea cup and looked at Eleanor thoughtfully. "This is very unexpected news, Eleanor."

She looked back at him. "Yes, uncle. I'm afraid it must seem a bit sudden."

"I know you to be a sensible young woman but from what I understand, you know little about this Mr Henshaw," said her uncle.

"I believe I know enough, Uncle Arthur," she replied.

"Hmm. I see. And we must assume that you have given this proposal proper consideration and it is what you desire," he said.

"Yes. It is, Uncle," she said.

Arthur stood up. "In that case, Eleanor, I wish you well and offer my sincere congratulations."

He glanced across at his wife's concerned face and smiled reassuringly. "Well, I'm sure you ladies have plenty to discuss. I'll be in my study, Joan."

Martha, Arthur and Joan's daughter, sat beside Eleanor on the sofa. She was two years younger than

Eleanor and since childhood they had been devoted to one another. She took hold of Eleanor's hand. "Do you love this man, Eleanor?" she asked.

"Henry has been very supportive. He is dependable," said Eleanor,

Martha gave a short laugh. "Dependable, eh? Oh Eleanor, what's that got to do with love?"

"He seems to be a good man. They say that love can grow, Martha," said Eleanor, levelly.

Joan looked at her niece gravely. "And what about your mother? What does she have to say?" she asked.

"Mama considers it an excellent match. In fact the news has given her a new lease of life, Aunt Joan," said Eleanor.

"I see. I suppose my sister sees advantages in this match." said Joan.

Eleanor nodded. "We won't have to sell the house, Aunt Joan. Mama can continue to live in the way to which she is accustomed."

Joan grunted and turned away, muttering to herself about her sister's spoilt and selfish nature.

Martha looked at Eleanor earnestly. "Oh, dearest Eleanor, are you really sure you have thought this through?"

"You've always told me I have an impetuous nature, haven't you Martha? But, believe me, I haven't come to this decision lightly," said Eleanor.

Joan turned back to her niece. "We've heard little from you about the immediate circumstances that have brought you to this decision, but your uncle and I have a fair idea of what has taken place. I want you to know that we consider you to be a very loyal, brave girl, if not a little proud."

Martha got up and started to pace the room. "But Eleanor, what about Declan? You've said nothing about him. Surely he won't allow you to do this?" she said.

Eleanor bit down hard on her lower lip. "Declan has been told." She didn't mention that she had been up all night after accepting Henry's proposal, agonising over the letter she eventually sent, nor of its consequences. She couldn't tell Martha of his visit to the house and the painful exchange that ensued when Declan refused to accept her rejection of him until she forced herself to tell him that what had taken place between them was no more than infatuation

Hearing the heated exchange between them Melanie had entered the room. "Dear Declan, I think you should behave like a gentleman and accept my daughter's decision," she said to him, sweetly.

He glared at her. "Gentleman be damned!"

Eleanor wanted to scream at her mother to mind her own business and to tell him that she loved him but Declan was gone.

Aunt Joan looked at her sadly. "Oh child, you are not yet nineteen years old."

At that moment Eleanor felt a great deal older. She gave her aunt a small smile. "I am engaged to be married, Aunt Joan. Please try to be happy for me."

After Eleanor left them Joan and her daughter stared at each other in dismay. "I fear that there is no way to stop this happening, however wrong it seems. Oh, the poor lamb!" said Joan.

"Oh, Mother, don't!" cried Martha and burst into tears.

Chapter 9

Alice sat down heavily on the stair at the foot of the staircase. She rested her elbows on her knees and held her head between her hands. What was happening to her? The visions of those past lives had evaporated yet she was still in their thrall. She was so embroiled in Eleanor's world it felt as though she herself was inside it, both as observer and witness to the events that took place. There had to be a reason for the phenomenon and she couldn't shrink from it. Eleanor needed to share her story and she herself must wait for it to unfold.

Close by, an insistent voice penetrated her thoughts and she felt a hand on her arm. "Alice!"

She opened her eyes and saw Tom frowning at her.

"Alice, I'm bored," he said.

Alice looked up at the two children standing in front her. "Oh, I thought you were outside with Damien."

"He's gone. He had stuff to do in town," said Poppy.

"Can't we go up to the tower? You keep promising," said Tom.

Tom had been pleading to go up to the tower for days and Alice remembered Kate had given her the key for the door to the stairway. This seemed like a good moment to do so.

The door to the tower was in the stone vestibule at the end of the attic corridor and Alice turned the key in the lock. Behind the door was a spiral stairway with steep narrow steps and she warned the children to tread carefully before they started the climb. At the top they found themselves in a low-ceilinged circular room. It was cold and dingy with small slit windows set high in the walls that provided scant light and little warmth from the sunshine outside.

Tom jumped up and down on the filthy old mattress that lay discarded on the floor. "This is wicked!"

Poppy stared at the mattress with distaste. "Does somebody sleep in here?"

"We could sleep here. It would be so cool!" said Tom.

"Oh, no!" said Poppy in horror. She edged closer to Alice. "It's spooky!"

Alice put an arm around her and glanced around the dingy room. "No one is going to sleep in here, Poppy. It's much too dirty and damp."

The door onto the parapet was so stiff and unwieldy that it took several pushes to force it open. On the other side of the doorway was the large circular parapet enclosed in low granite walls. Tom raced around it and when he returned Alice caught hold of his arm.

"No running, Tom!"

He went to the wall and stared out. "This is where we can spy out the enemy!"

Poppy and Alice stood beside him. Alice looked down at the steep drop. "Careful there, don't lean over the edge," she said.

"We could shoot cannon balls at them, and if anyone tries to get in, we'll pour down vats of boiling tar," Tom said, laughing gleefully.

The views were spectacular. "Look, over there you can even see the town!" said Alice, pointing in the distance.

"That's not a town, Alice," said Tom. "That's the Roman army coming to invade us."

"What! The Roman army here!" said Alice, aghast.

"Yes, quick. We'd best defend ourselves," said Tom.

"With our superior arsenal of weaponry, we'll soon send that army into retreat," said Alice.

"Yes, yes, prepare for an attack!" Tom commanded, withdrawing an imaginary spear from its quiver.

Alice was relaxed and enjoying the game until suddenly she sensed something menacing and sinister lurking in the tower that filled her with dread. The fear she felt was connected to Eleanor and her pulse began to race.

Poppy looked up at her. "What's the matter, Alice?"

Surprised by the child's acuity, Alice looked down with a reassuring smile. "Just a funny turn, Poppy. I'll be fine in a moment."

She didn't want Poppy alarmed by her panic attack, or the compulsion to flee that accompanied it.

"I expect you're like Mummy. She doesn't like heights, either," said Poppy.

"Yes, you're right, Poppy," said Alice. She turned to Tom. "That's enough for now, Tom. It's time to go."

"But look, Alice, look!" he cried, pointing to the bottom of the driveway. "We can't go yet. The enemy's almost at the gates."

Alice took hold of his arm. "Come on, Tom. Dave will be waiting. He said he'd be at the lake today."

As they re-entered the circular room, Tom glanced around jubilantly. "Look Alice, we can keep our prisoners in here for years and years and no one will ever know they're here!"

Alice shuddered at the thought. "No, I dare say, Tom. But we're taking no prisoners today."

That afternoon Dave had a surprise for Tom. He had brought along the Japanese warship he had just finished painting and Alice sat with Poppy on the embankment watching it set off on its maiden voyage.

Poppy turned to Alice with an earnest gaze. "Alice, can I ask you a question?"

"Of course. What is it?"

"Why did you come into our room last night?"

"Just to check you were okay."

"But why were you crying?"

"I wasn't crying, Poppy."

Poppy continued as though she hadn't heard Alice. "And you were wearing such a beautiful dress! I loved the way it rustled when you moved. I thought you had been to a party."

Alice shook her head. "No. There was no party."

"Then it must have been that other lady."

"What other lady?"

"I don't know her name. But she was wearing this lovely long dress and she had a big straw hat."

Alice look at her anxiously. "Where did you meet this lady, Poppy?"

"That day we came here with Erin. She walked past me while you were talking."

"And did she speak to you?"

"No. She just vanished into the woods."

Alice put a hand on her shoulder. "So she didn't bother you?"

"Oh, no. She was nice."

On her return from London, Kate told Alice that she had arranged a small celebration for Ben's thirtieth birthday and that evening they went for dinner at the Smugglers Retreat, a beautiful seventeenth-century inn in the next village.

"Jack, the new proprietor, used to be head chef at the Savoy so the food should be excellent. Just as well to check out the competition!" she said.

Ben arrived alone. He told Alice later he had just met someone he liked very much. She was a nurse and that evening was working a night shift.

The meal was as good as Kate had predicted but afterwards the evening went downhill. Kate's announcement that she had accepted the job of consultant to the management at the Manville did not receive the reception she had expected.

"Kate, you can't be serious?" said Ben.

"I certainly am. They need me there. Standards have deteriorated and some of our clients have started going elsewhere," she said. "The offer comes with a very lucrative deal, too."

"What about Langsmead?" asked Julian.

"It won't affect my work there. I'll be up in town during the two-day break," said Kate.

"But you'll burn yourself out," said Julian. "Are you sure about this, Kate?"

"Yes, of course I am. It's a marvellous opportunity," said Kate.

Julian raised his eyebrows at Ben.

"Sounds crazy to me," said Ben.

"Well, thanks for the support, guys," Kate said, crossly.

At the end of the meal Jack came to their table to see Kate. They talked for a good half hour and when he left she handed him one of her cards.

"Poor Jack is in a mess. He needs a manager," she said later, while they walked across the car park to the car.

Ben and Julian looked at each other and rolled their eyes

Back at the house, they sat in the sitting room drinking the bottle of vintage champagne that Kate produced from the cellar. Ben had Alice in stitches describing some of the eccentricities of his wealthy clients, but the champagne had not improved Kate's mood.

"What's up with you, Kate?" she heard Julian ask.

"I thought you'd be pleased for me. It's a great career move."

"Oh, for God's sake, Kate. Why does it matter what Ben or I think or anyone else at the end of the day? It's your decision. Your life."

"It should matter," said Kate.

"Come on, Kate, you're just overtired," he said.

She muttered something at him and stood up. "I'm off to bed."

"Don't break up the party, Kate. It's my birthday!" said Ben.

"I'm sorry, Ben, but I'm a busy working woman," she said. "Loads to do tomorrow including a visit from the film company."

Alice thought it politic for her to leave and got up, too.

"You don't have to go, too, do you, Alice?" Ben asked tipsily, waving the champagne bottle at her. "There's still half a bottle left."

Julian winked at Ben. "It's what they call female solidarity, Ben."

Chapter 10

Suzie and several other employees turned up for work in the morning although officially it was a day off. Suzie remarked that it wasn't every day they had the chance to meet people from the telly.

Suzie was expecting glamour and was very disappointed when she set eyes on Angela Marsden, head of the production team. Angela was a woman of indeterminate age with a brusque and business-like manner. She had short cropped hair and the tight jeans she wore with her t-shirt did little to enhance her pear-shaped figure. However, Suzie's eyes did brighten when she saw the director, Sebastian Seth-Smith. He was young and good looking and, according to Suzie, his easy charm more than compensated for his colleague's deficiency. Suzie said he had the bluest eyes she had ever seen and by the end of the day the female staff were smitten.

Alice witnessed little of the visit, but when she returned from a picnic by the lake with the children Suzie was bursting with gossip.

"Do you know, he really took a shine to Kate," she said. "After I served them lunch the old bag left the table to make a phone call or something and he and Kate started talking really intimately. The way he looked at her made me green with envy!"

Kate looked much more cheerful afterwards when she told Alice how successful the visit had been. She seemed to have made peace with Julian, but Alice did start to question their relationship, particularly after being witness to another hostile exchange a few days later.

It was a Sunday morning and she was with Kate in the sitting room. Julian was seated in an armchair reading The Times when Kate put aside the supplement she was reading and started leafing through her diary. "My God, Ascot's almost upon us and I haven't even got an outfit sorted."

She glanced across at Julian. "Julian, Ascot's in ten days' time."

He didn't look up. "Oh?"

"The Broadbanks have invited us to share their box on Ladies' Day." she said.

Julian turned the page of his newspaper. "I'd rather give it a miss, Kate."

"But you can't, they're expecting us."

"Then make an excuse," he said.

She stared across at him. "I thought you enjoyed it last year."

He said nothing and Kate looked irritated. "Julian, you know how much I love Ascot!"

"Well, there's nothing to prevent you from going, is there?" he said.

Kate was ready with a sharp retort but instead she changed tack. She went across the room and perched on the arm of his chair. "Oh come on, darling, Sarah and Colin are great fans of yours, you know," she said, ruffling his hair.

He brushed off her hand as though it were a fly. "One day with Sarah and Colin was enough for me."

Kate stood up and stared down at him. "I thought it was fun."

"That couple are about as much fun as a wet afternoon on Bognor Regis seafront."

Kate's voice grew shrill. "Please don't insult my friends!"

Alice made a hasty exit and went to find Tom and Poppy in the orchard. It was almost time to take them over to the Johnsons. The boys' mother had phoned to invite Tom for lunch and said that her seven-year-old daughter would love the chance to meet Poppy.

"We're up here, Alice," Poppy called from the upper branch of an apple tree.

Alice stood at the bottom of the tree. "Come down now, it's time to go."

Tom slipped down the tree with the agility of a monkey and dropped down beside Alice. She glanced at his torn t-shirt. "You'll have to get changed, Tom," she said and held up a hand to help Poppy down. Tom groaned.

"You can't go out to lunch like that!" she said and dragged him back to the house.

There was silence from the sitting room when Alice returned from dropping off the children in the village. She found a novel of Julian's on the library shelf and took it out to the terrace.

She had just started reading when Kate appeared. "That man's been so bloody minded lately," she said, clonking down on a chair. "Why on earth has he stopped wanting to socialise?"

"Maybe he's just preoccupied with his novel."

"Well, screw him!" said Kate watching the couple who were strolling across the lawn.

Each carried a tennis racket and the man had his arm around his female companion. As they came closer Alice saw that he was in late middle age and sported a perma-tan. His trendy sports gear promoted a youthful image and the leggy young blonde woman compounded the ruse.

"There are other fish in the sea."

Alice crinkled her nose in distaste. "You don't mean him, I hope."

"No, no, that's Gary Holmes, the photographer. He's here to take publicity shots. It was quite a scoop getting him, but Gary's returning a favour."

"Looks like he's got a penchant for pubescent girls anyway," said Alice.

"The fish I have in mind is considerably younger and better looking," said Kate.

"Who are you talking about?"

"A young film director called Se-ba-sti-an," said Kate, drawing out the syllables in his name.

"Oh, that TV bloke who was here the other day?"

She nodded. "He's invited me out, you know."

"Are you going?"

"I'm thinking about it. A little competition might wake Julian up."

Alice didn't agree but decided not to argue the point.

Kate didn't mention Sebastian again for several weeks and in the meantime Alice noticed her distancing herself from Julian. She went to Ascot alone, accepting his absence without further comment. Nor did she make any objection to Julian's decision to join the golf club though she did remark upon his absences.

"How come he's never here when I'm here?" she said one afternoon. "I got back early so we could spend some time together."

"Maybe he didn't know you were coming," said Alice.

"Oh he knew," she said. "I'm getting so pissed off, you know. He's either hidden away in the study or swinging a bloody golf club."

"Then talk to him about it."

Kate's eyes were glistening. She pulled a tissue from her bag and blew her nose. "It's so bloody hurtful, but I just can't go crawling to him again."

Following their first visit to the club house it had become a regular event for Alice to take the children to meet Julian after his game. If Kate was too proud to tell him how hurt she was Alice decided to do so herself. One afternoon as they were having a lager at the bar she mentioned that Kate was upset that she saw him so rarely.

He stared at her for a moment and grinned. "Well, it's your fault that I've taken up golf again, you know."

"What?"

"Well, you were responsible for coercing me into playing with that Brewster bloke. Were it not for that, my clubs might have remained in their bag indefinitely."

Alice sighed in defeat.

"Anyway why aren't you or the kids complaining?" he said. "If I wasn't such a selfish bastard, I'd be spending the time with them."

"Oh, you know how much they love coming here and have you indulge them with all those crisps and fizzy drinks," she said, glancing across at Tom and Poppy who were playing on the fruit machines. "Just look at them. Those machines are as addictive as your golf clubs."

Julian turned to talk to another member and Nigel, his golfing partner, approached. "Good to see you again, Alice," he said smiling.

Nigel was an affable, personable man in his early forties who regularly joined her for a chat.

"How are you, Nigel?" asked Alice.

"Business is booming," he said with a grin.

Nigel had confided in her about his unsatisfactory domestic situation, his wife having absconded to the south of France with their children. Alice asked after them.

"Penny says they're on an extended holiday."

"Why don't you go over and bring them back?"

"Oh, I don't want her back and I told her so. But I do want the kids. I phone them every evening and my boy Justin talks all the time about a bloke called Pierre. When I asked Penny about him she said he was her personal trainer."

"Maybe he is."

"More likely any activity which takes place happens in the bedroom."

"All the more reason to go and find out."

He shook his head. "Nah, I'm leaving that to the private detective. He'll find out soon enough."

He gestured to the barman to serve them another drink. "I tell you something, Alice, when I see you and the kids, I'm so envious. Julian doesn't know what a lucky blighter he is!"

It took a moment for Alice to realise what he meant. "Oh my God, I'm afraid you've got the wrong end of the stick. The children are Julian's nephew and niece."

"Oh, is that so?" He paused for a moment. "So it's just you and him then?"

Nigel was the second person to assume that Julian and Alice were a couple. It was disconcerting. "No, Nigel. Julian is just a friend. He's the boyfriend of my best friend Kate. She's the manager at Langsmead Hall."

Nigel grinned. "Well I'll be damned. That does change the picture!"

Poppy tugged at Alice's sleeve. "Alice, Tom's spent all the money and I've only had one go."

"I'll see if I've got any change," said Alice, reaching for her bag.

"Here, I've got some," said Nigel, scooping out a handful of coins from his trouser pocket. He held them out in the palm of his hand. "Now, take what you need, young lady."

Poppy scampered off, clutching a fistful of coins.

"That's very good of you," said Alice.

"No, no, she's a cute little girl, whether she's yours or not." He took a long drink of his beer. "You give this image of the perfect little nuclear family, you know. I'm amazed Julian didn't put me right, but then he's an odd bloke, rarely talks about himself."

"Hmm. Quite an unusual quality in a man."

"Ooh, ouch!"

Alice chuckled. "Nothing personal intended."

"I still reckon the old bugger should have told me. I thought we were mates."

"Told you what?"

"That you weren't an item, of course."

"It was you that made that assumption, Nigel."

"Okay, you've made your point," he grinned. "But you are living up at the hotel, aren't you?"

"Yes, I'm there for the summer."

"You know, I put in an offer for Langsmead Hall myself but got outbid by that hotel consortium."

"And what did you propose to do with it?"

"The area would have gained much-needed new housing."

"In that case, I'm very glad you didn't succeed!"

"Well, that sounded heartfelt," he said. "Do I take it that you have an investment at stake?"

Alice shook her head. "No, nothing like that. I just believe it would be sheer vandalism to destroy such a wonderful old house."

"At the end of the day, these large properties don't pay for themselves. And I've got my doubts that your Langsmead Hall will prove to be a commercial success."

"Now you're depressing me."

He put his hand on hers and gave a flirty smile. "Then I'm sorry. That's the last thing I'd want, Alice."

Alice glanced across the room and caught Julian's eye. "It's time to get the children back," she mouthed, pointing at her watch.

Nigel followed them out of the club house. "You know what, old man, one of these days I'm going to break that horrible swing of yours!" he said, slinging an arm around Julian's shoulder.

The two men stopped for a moment beside Nigel's sleek E-type Jaguar.

As Julian followed the Jaguar out of the car park, he turned to Alice in the passenger seat beside him. "You've made a hit there, Alice. Nigel's taken a real fancy to you."

Alice groaned.

"He has it in mind to ask you out." said Julian.

"I'm afraid Nigel's been under a lot of misapprehensions and evidently still is."

"What do you mean?"

"I don't go out with married men. Let's leave it at that."

"By all accounts, he won't be for much longer."

"And you think I'd want to get mixed up in a messy divorce?"

"Oh, don't be so hasty, Alice. Nigel's the local property magnate. The guy's loaded, you know."

"I really don't give a damn how loaded he is and you can just stop winding me up!" she said.

From the back seat came titters of laughter. Alice turned around and glared at Tom and Poppy. "And you know what they say about eavesdroppers, don't you? Their ears drop off!"

Kate was in the kitchen when they got back and as Alice came into the room, she looked up from the pan she was stirring. "Ah, you're back at last! Where's Julian?"

"I think they went into the library. Julian's promised to teach Tom how to play snooker," said Alice, giving Kate a peck on the cheek. "This is a nice surprise, we weren't expecting you till later."

"As you see, I'm still making an effort," she said, removing the wooden spoon from the pan. "I suppose you were up at the golf club."

"Uh huh. It's time you went up there, Kate."

"Maybe one of these days," she said. She went across to the sideboard and picked up her cigarettes. "I think I need an early night. I don't get enough of them these days."

Alice inspected the contents of the pan that was simmering on the Aga. "Is this a Bolognese sauce?"

"Yes. I think you said the kids liked it so I asked Maria to knock some up."

Tom came into the room and ran up to Alice. "Is supper ready yet? I'm starving!"

"And where are your manners, young man?" said Alice, nodding towards Kate.

Tom turned to her and gave a quick smile. "Hallo, Kate."

Kate smiled back. "Good evening, Tom."

"Kate's got your favourite supper. It'll be ready in ten minutes," said Alice, loading spaghetti into a pan of boiling water. "Go and get Poppy, will you? And tell Julian that Kate's here."

Kate stared at Tom's retreating figure. "That was impressive! He really looks quite sweet when he smiles."

Poppy sat down at the table opposite Kate. "Alice has got a date," she said.

Kate raised her eyebrows. "Oh?"

"That's not true!" said Alice, indignantly.

"His name's Nigel. He fancies her," said Poppy, solemnly digging a fork into her plate of spaghetti.

"The guy's loaded, you know!" said Tom.

Both children burst into a fit of giggles. Alice scowled at them. "That's quite enough!"

Kate turned to her. "What have I been missing?"

"Nothing, Kate. They're just being silly!"

"Well, if you ask me, the guy sounds like good news. I'd like to meet him," said Kate, laughing.

Chapter 11

The month of July had come in with a heatwave and one scorching day followed another.

"Thank God we got the air conditioning installed in time," said Kate, glancing around the cool dining room. "If I'd had my way, we'd have had the swimming pool built by now." She turned to Alice. "Where are the kids by the way? They're usually attached to you at the hip."

"Oh, they were up really early and had their breakfast in the kitchen. I'm planning on taking them to the coast today. The pool in town is really crowded," said Alice.

"Hmm, good idea," said Kate, helping herself to toast.

Julian appeared at the table and pulled up a chair. "Did I hear something about a trip to the coast?"

"I thought you were working?" said Kate

"It's too hot. That study is stifling," he said. "A trip to the seaside is a splendid idea. Why don't we all go?"

"You can count me out, Julian. I'd only get burnt to a frazzle," Kate said.

Suzie told them about a secluded beach she knew and an hour later they were out in the driveway ready to depart. Kate brought out a picnic hamper and they loaded it into the boot of Julian's car.

"I wish you'd change your mind, Kate," said Alice.

"And come back looking like a freshly cooked lobster, no thanks! You know what my skin is like," said Kate. "I may pop over to the Norfolk Arms to see Jack if I get a moment."

"Oh, don't you ever stop?"

Julian came up and gave Kate's cheek a peck. "She doesn't know how!"

The beach was situated at the end of a long rutted track "God knows what this road has done to my tyres," said Julian as they finally reached its end and he parked the car in an area of scrub by the edge of some cliffs.

"Oh, but look at this, Julian!" said Alice. "I think you'll decide it was worth it."

She stood with the children looking down at the bay that nestled amongst a circle of tall cliffs. The tide was up and the azure sea that lapped the shore beckoned enticingly. There were a handful of families scattered across the narrow stretch of exposed beach and the children couldn't wait to scramble down the narrow path.

When Julian challenged Alice to swim out to the raft that bobbed on the water a few hundred yards from the shore, she didn't hesitate. Much to his chagrin, she reached the raft and was already afloat when he approached.

"My God, you didn't tell me you were in training for the Olympics!" he gasped, taking in a mouthful of sea water. Alice laughed and dived back into the water.

His head emerged from the wave she created and holding onto the raft with one hand he raised his fist with the other. "Nor did I realise you were such an exhibitionist!" he yelled out.

All tension seemed to have been expunged from Alice's body and she was feeling that sense of exhilaration that happens after an invigorating swim. Even that ever present preoccupation with Eleanor didn't disturb her equanimity. She spread out her beach towel, lay down on the sand. She was just dozing off when Julian's voice stirred her into consciousness. He was saying something about the strength of the sun. Suddenly, she remembered the children and was wide awake. She grabbed up hats, t-shirts and sun cream and flew down the beach.

Alice had left them playing in the emerging rock pools, but the tide had receded, leaving a wide stretch of wet brown sand on which they were playing a game of rounders with a group of other children. She coaxed Tom and Poppy into their t-shirts and dabbed sun cream on their faces before they rushed off again.

There were two adults supervising the game and one of them handed the baton to Tom. Alice stayed to watch his performance. He hit the ball with an almighty slam and it flew through the air, skimming Alice's nose by inches. She took a step backwards and found Julian behind her.

"A close one!" he laughed and handed over her cotton sarong. "I thought you might need this."

She tied it around her and they hung about watching for a while.

"It feels as hot as the Caribbean today," said Alice as they walked back to their patch. "I remember getting burnt there on my first day and spent the next one in bed."

"Where were you?" he asked.

"Tobago," she said.

"I know Tobago. We went there on our honeymoon, Anna and I," he said.

"And I was there with Richard," said Alice. "It was our first holiday together."

Julian put up the hotel parasol that Kate had insisted they take with them and they sat down by the huge boulders that nestled in the sand.

"Is Richard the bloke you were living with?" he asked.

"Yes. We were together almost twelve years."

"Sounds more like a marriage."

Alice felt a moment of bitterness "Hmm. A barren marriage you might call it."

"Maybe just as well there were no children, as things turned out."

"I didn't think so at the time."

Alice thought of her excitement the first time she got pregnant. "There's plenty of time to start thinking about a family. Aren't we happy as we are?' is what he had said. She was too much in his thrall to dispute his perspective and agreed upon a termination.

Julian handed her a drink from the cold box. "Was Richard that guy you were with when we met?"

She nodded.

"You didn't look very happy," he said.

"No. It was just before we split up," she said. "Of course, it hadn't always been like that. I was happy enough at first. He was a successful producer then, in fact he was riding high at the Beeb."

"Did you work there, too?"

"No. It was in the days when Kate and I had our little catering business. We prepared a buffet for his thirtieth birthday party. That's how we first met."

"Does Richard still work at the Beeb?"

"No, he left years ago to start up his own production company."

"A brave step!"

"A foolhardy one, as it turned out. Within two years the company had to go into liquidation. His major backers had reneged on a deal and were withholding any more finance. The next blow came when I discovered he had borrowed heavily on the house. I was five months pregnant at the time." She picked up a handful of sand and watched it slip through her fingers. "But then I contracted shingles and lost the baby. The doctor said it was due to stress."

He was silent for a moment and she watched Tom and Poppy playing tag on the sand.

"Why didn't you leave him?" he asked.

"It's complicated."

On the day she came home from hospital Richard had been in rehab for a week and the house was empty. There was no baby, no partner, no money and unless some action was taken soon there would be no house. There was nowhere to go but upwards. The house was an average 1930s semi in a leafy street in Twickenham and since her grandmother died it had been her only home.

Alice had arrived at a crossroads. She could pack a bag and walk away, leaving the past behind, but as she wandered through the rooms that they had renovated and refurbished with such care and love, she reached a decision. She would find herself a better paid job, a much better paid job. It was in the classified section of *The Times* that she came across a vacancy for a PA placed by a well-known pop star. She telephoned the number in the advertisement and was offered an immediate interview. The job came with an extremely high salary. The catch was that the post needed to be filled urgently. The prospective employee must be ready to start work the following week and be prepared to travel. After a moment's hesitation she decided there was nothing to lose.

"Go on, try me," said Julian.

"I didn't know that it had all gone belly up until a couple of months after we returned from a visit to my mother in Cape Town. Richard had started drinking heavily and he took full advantage of the cheap booze over there. Mum never mentioned it, but I suspect he came up with one of his grand schemes and tried to borrow money from her. I knew they had fallen out but all Mum said was that I should find myself someone more reliable."

"She may have had a point," Julian said.

Alice nodded and smiled ruefully. "One day Richard collapsed in the street. Our doctor referred him to a rehab clinic and I landed a job with Ron Humphrey."

Julian laughed. "What, Ron Humphrey the pop star! You worked for him!"

"Yes, I was his PA for five years. What's so funny about that?"

"I can't imagine you involved in the pop scene!"

"I was only on the periphery. In fact, Ron was a very good employer, extremely generous, too."

"You're made of sterner stuff than I realised."

She grinned. "Just stubborn!"

It was early evening by the time they returned to the hotel. The new guests had arrived and the place was buzzing with activity. Alice settled the children upstairs and after a bath and quick change of clothes, she went to the drawing room for the cocktail hour. Kate stood near the entrance welcoming the guests as they came into the room. Julian wasn't there and Kate looked pleased to see her. She introduced Alice to the attractive young couple she was talking to.

"This is Lori and Harvey Rubinstein. They're from New York and Lori's parents are regulars at the Manville," said Kate. She flashed a smile at them and turned away.

Alice learned from Lori, a pretty dark-haired girl, that they had only been married for one week and that their visit to England was a wedding present from her parents. She slipped her arm into Harvey's. "I've dreamed of coming to England ever since I was in school, haven't I, honey?" she said, glancing up at Harvey adoringly.

He smiled indulgently. "To tell you the truth, Alice, I didn't even know that England had countryside! This trip has been quite a revelation!"

Lori turned to him and laughed. "Oh Harvey, you never told me that!"

He turned doting eyes on her and kissed the tip of her nose. "Of course I didn't. Had you known of my ignorance, you might never have married me!"

"Yeah, right, such a gap in your education is quite unforgivable!" she said with a giggle.

"And another thing I'm impressed with is your weather, Alice," he said. "I was told it always rained here!"

It may have been because the young newly-weds had been deprived of other company for the last week and wanted a sounding board for their impressions of British culture that it became difficult for Alice to detach herself. As she listened to them she tried to recall what it was like to be so in love and found herself wondering whether their love would stay the course. Life was ephemeral and fortune could be fickle. Suzie approached with a tray of drinks and Alice picked up another champagne cocktail to toast their future happiness.

Julian did not appear at Kate's soirée but joined them later in the dining room.

"You're late. I'm afraid we've started," Kate said as he came to the table.

"Yes, I apologise," he said, taking a seat. "I was upstairs watching TV with Tom and Poppy. I didn't realise the time."

"So how was the trip to the seaside?" Kate asked him.

"It was extremely enjoyable," he said. He turned to Alice and winked. "Full of surprises, too."

Kate noticed Alice toying with her food. "What's wrong with your starter, Ali?"

"I think I drank too much," she said.

"All the more reason to get some food inside you," said Kate.

Alice twiddled with the stem of her wine glass "I was chatting to that young honeymoon couple…"

"Oh yes, aren't they sweet?" said Kate.

Victor came up to the table to serve their entrée. Kate eyed the plump Dover souls that he held aloft. "Fresh from Hastings this morning!" she said to us. "Hmm, they look cooked to perfection. Thank you, Victor."

Alice stared at her plate in dismay. She could feel tears slipping down her face and saw them form droplets on the parsley butter. "I'm sorry Kate, but I don't think I can eat this."

She didn't remember what followed.

The next morning Kate appeared in Alice's bedroom.

"I've brought you some tea," she said, putting down a mug on the bedside table.

Alice stared at her in bemusement. "Oh God, have I overslept?"

"Not to worry," said Kate, going to the window and sweeping back the curtains. "The kids are having breakfast with Julian in the dining room. From what I could see, Tom's ordered everything on the menu!"

Alice sat up in bed feeling woozy. Flashes from the previous evening came back to her and she had a hazy memory of Kate helping her to bed. "Oh God, I was drunk!"

Kate sat down on the end of the bed. "It happens to the best of us," she said with a grin. "As a matter of fact, you were as sick as a dog when I finally managed to get you up here so I expect you got it all out of your system."

"Oh, Kate. I'm so sorry." said Alice, shaking her head in self-disgust. "I talked to Julian about Richard. What happened five years ago came flooding back as though it was yesterday."

"Delayed grief, I expect. I told you to get counselling after you lost the baby but instead you go rushing headlong into that job with Humphrey!"

An appalling thought entered Alice's head. "Did I make a spectacle of myself in the dining room?"

Kate laughed. "No. You actually made a surprisingly dignified exit. And as for making spectacles of ourselves, you really can't compete."

Alice took a long drink of tea and the fog began to recede.

"Remember that scene I made in the Savoy bar?" said Kate. "I don't know what I might have done had you not been there to restrain me."

Alice could not forget that traumatic evening when Kate's lover had broken off their relationship. She and the Honourable Anthony Cartwright MP had been having an intense affair for two years when he had suddenly dropped the bombshell.

"At least you had the presence of mind to phone me," said Alice.

"That must have been my strong sense of self-preservation kicking in!" Kate chuckled. "If it hadn't been for your intervention, I'd have gone straight round to their house and told his wife what a shit she was married to, not to mention being blacklisted from the Savoy for life!"

She went across to open the window and lit a cigarette. "As I said last night, you're not the only one to be naïve. I believed every word that lying bastard uttered, wedding bells and the whole bit. Then, out of the blue, my unhappily married lover tells me he's going back to his pregnant wife. Is that a cliché or not?"

Alice got out of bed and went to stand beside her.

"And every time I see his bloody picture in the papers I still get mad. And they say that time is a healer!"

In the distance, Alice glimpsed a familiar figure walking across the kitchen garden. "Just look at Dave. Now there goes a person content with his lot. Why can't we all be like him?"

"What, make our living by tending the soil. God forbid!" said Kate, laughing.

Chapter 12

As Alice walked with the children through the garden the next morning, Tom spotted Dave inside the fruit cage and he ran over to meet him. "Morning, Miss," said Dave. He was carrying a basket half filled with raspberries as he came out with Tom.

Alice told him they were on their way to the lake.

"Not sure I'll be along. Got a lot to get done today," he said.

"Oh, please come, Dave," said Tom.

He scratched his head. "Got all them weeds in there to sort out. Soon as me back is turned they're there again."

Tom was eyeing the raspberries covetously. "We could help you, Dave."

Dave held out the basket. "You can fill this up, if you like."

Tom darted off with Poppy on his heels. "And don't eat too many," said Alice.

"Them two's the right size for that job," said Dave, stretching out his back. "We've a grand crop this year. I doubt a few gone missing'll be noticed."

Alice spent so many of her waking hours thinking about Eleanor that she needed to know what had happened to her and why she herself had this extraordinary connection. With Tom and Poppy happily occupied she took the opportunity to question Dave.

He took a tin of tobacco from his pocket and rolled a cigarette. "All I know is what my Gran told me about the lady. Gran first came to these parts the year after the start of the Great War when she was employed as maid to Miss Maude Henshaw, the mistress's sister-in-law."

"So your grandmother was working at the house?"

"No, she arrived the day that them youngsters were drowned. The housekeeper had telephoned Miss Henshaw 'cause the young mistress was away and she came to take charge."

"Do you know how it happened, Dave?"

"It happened ever so quick, according to my Gran. One minute they were playing on the bank and the next they were gone. Reckon they'd have been about the same age as them two in there."

Alice shuddered. "Poor Eleanor."

He nodded. "By all accounts she was a lovely lady."

She asked him whether there was anyone else she could talk to about Eleanor.

He took a long draw on his cigarette. "I reckon Miss Ellen Henshaw would be the only one. She's the last of the family left."

"She was the former owner of the house?"

"Yes, Miss Henshaw is living in the village now. God bless her," said Dave.

Whilst waiting for Dave, Tom sat on the river bank, his fishing rod dipped into the lake. Poppy sat next to him watching the fish that darted around his lure. Alice was seated on a rug under a nearby oak. She had opened her book and was starting to read when something made her look up. On the opposite side of the lake a figure appeared through the trees. For a moment it halted as though to survey the landscape. A shaft of sunlight slanted through the foliage, illuminating the silhouette in a golden aura. It was Julian.

Poppy spotted him and ran over. She jumped up into his arms and he tossed her up in the air. Alice put away her book and watched Julian grab hold of an arm and a leg and whiz Poppy round and round until, with shrieks of laughter, she collapsed in a heap on the grass. He pulled her up and they went over to Tom.

Julian had brought along Dave's speedboat and he crouched down beside Tom on the bank until the boat was ejected onto the water. Alice smiled, thinking idly about what a good father he would make. If she were Kate, she would never let this man go.

Julian waved to her and a few minutes later he strolled over. "Hello, there."

Alice smiled up at him. "This is a nice surprise."

He gestured to the rug. "May I join you?"

"Of course. This is my favourite spot, you know," she said, drawing up her outstretched legs. "I can see the whole lake from here, and keep an eye on the children."

"I've come as Dave's substitute today," he said, sitting down. "When I returned from a trip to buy ink cartridges, Dave caught me in the driveway. He said he couldn't come and asked if I'd mind bringing along the boat for Tom."

"No golf then?"

He shook his head. "No. High time I spent more time with the kids, don't you think? And well, the opportunity arose," he said with a grin. "And how are we feeling today Alice?"

Alice was embarrassed by the unspoken reminder of the previous evening. She rolled her eyes. "I'm well, thank you."

He gestured at the book that poked out of her basket. "What are you reading?"

"It's one of yours actually," she said, picking up the book. "I'm on the last few chapters."

He took the book from her and looked at the title. "Ah, *The Lion's Den*. That was my third."

Alice nodded "Yes. I've been reading them in the sequence they were written and I think I like this one most. Kate's got them all in library."

He grinned. "They're not compulsory reading, you know."

"No, but they are addictive. I like the pace you set. It really keeps you on your toes," she said, flicking through the book. "I've just got to the bit when Jake discovers that Annie's a terrorist and they're actually on opposing sides. How could an arch cynic like Jake be so taken in?"

"Then you're not convinced by her duplicity?"

"It's just so unexpected."

"Her husband was assassinated by the CIA."

"Yes, yes, it's totally plausible but how awful to be betrayed by the one person you've ever come to trust. Poor chap!"

"Don't they say that love is blind?"

"And all clichés are fundamentally true."

"Hmm. George Orwell." he said, leaning back against the tree and kicking off his shoes. "The fact is you can believe you know a person very well and feel really close to them yet then discover that you don't actually know them at all."

"I guess that's why human relationships are so complex," she said. "But now I come to think about it, there is something enigmatic about Annie's emotional response to him. It's like she's holding something back."

"People can be very good at leading a double life, you know. It happens more often than you'd think."

A silly idea came into her head. "Imagine if Kate had got involved in a terrorist cell and were up in London hatching nefarious plots. We'd be the last to suspect her!"

He laughed at the absurdity. "I doubt Kate has the time!"

"You know, Julian, it isn't a habit of mine to divulge the details of my personal life. I don't know what got into me yesterday."

He smiled. "It seemed perfectly natural to me."

His expression was serious in repose, but when he smiled, she noticed how the corners of his eyes crinkled up most appealingly.

"Perhaps as a policeman you got too used to being the interrogator."

"What's that supposed to mean, Alice?"

"You ask a lot of questions, but you never talk about yourself."

"You may have a point," he said with a chuckle.

"Don't you ever let down your guard?"

He turned to look at her. "I haven't always been like that."

"What changed?

"Something seemed to shut off after my wife died."

"Kate said that she was killed in a car accident."

"Yes. I was driving."

"Oh, God! How dreadful for you."

"I was given leave of absence but shortly afterwards I resigned."

"How long ago was that?"

"Ten years. I'd been with the Met for fifteen." He was silent for a while and stared out across the lake. "After Anna's death, my life came to a standstill. It happened so suddenly. One minute she was sitting beside me and we were chatting away and then this guy comes out onto the motorway and tries to overtake, smashing into the passenger side. There was nothing I could do, though afterwards I kept wondering whether my reactions had been quick enough."

He paused for a moment. "The other driver had hardly a scratch and my only injury was a dislocated shoulder."

"How did you deal with it?"

"After a couple of months, I packed a bag and bought a plane ticket to Australia. I needed to do something different and to be in some place where I could do my grieving in private."

"And was that cathartic?"

He nodded. "If you need to sort yourself out, you can't find a bigger or more faraway place to do it in. For days I drove through the Northern Territory with nothing but red earth stretching for hundreds and hundreds of miles."

"Did you stay long?"

"Yes, for several years. And I tried out a lot of things, from working on a sheep farm to reporting on a local rag. That's when I discovered I could write and I started to work on a novel. By the time I left, I had the first draft accepted in principle by an agent in England."

"Was that why you came back?"

"Not entirely. I got married again, you see. She was the daughter of the sheep farmer at the place where I was working. She was a pretty girl, but I think I was drunk when I proposed to her. She wasn't."

"So it didn't work out?"

"No, it was the most God-awful mistake. We were divorced several years ago. Fortunately, she met someone else, got married again and is very happy now."

"On the positive side, had you not gone to Australia you might never have discovered your writing talent. You might even have ended up as Police Commissioner instead!"

He chuckled. "No. I wasn't cut out to be a pen-pushing careerist."

"After fifteen years, it must have been a wrench."

"For most of my career I worked in the crime squad and was out there where the action was, not sitting behind a desk shuffling paper about like I did in Scotland Yard."

"Is that where you ended up?"

He nodded. "So, Alice, is the interrogation now over?"

"Almost," she said with a smile. "You hardly mentioned Anna before. What was she like?"

He looked out across the lake. "Anna was clever, witty and intuitive. Like you, she was a self-contained person."

He wanted to say more; to tell Alice how she had infiltrated the closed place in his heart and how lovely she looked at that moment. But he knew Alice well enough to know he must tread carefully. He was mulling it over when the children caught his attention. "Oh, look...what on earth is Tom up to?"

The doll was propped up on the motor boat and Tom propelled it out on the lake. The doll toppled into the water and Poppy let out a piercing shriek.

By now Alice was on her feet. "Oh, the silly boy!"

Poppy stood at the water's edge. "Miranda's drowning!" Poppy screamed in panic and Tom, armed with his fishing net, waded into the water.

"Stay where you are Poppy. I'll get your doll. You too, Tom, don't go any further," Julian called out and rushed across to them.

Alice was about to follow, but at that moment something happened that rooted her to the spot. The landscape was obscured by swirls of mist and through an iridescent haze she saw the figures of a boy and a girl hovering by the water at the end of the lake.

"Don't worry," the boy called. "I'll get her!"

He dived into the lake and the girl stood on the bank waiting for him, but moments passed and he didn't emerge. The water was silent and motionless. The girl called out to the boy, over and over again, and finally jumped in after him. The water closed over her.

The next moment Julian was walking towards Alice with Tom and Poppy beside him. A wet and bedraggled doll hung from Poppy's hand. It took a few moments for Alice to register them.

Poppy looked up at her earnestly and took hold of her hand. "Don't worry, Alice," she said. "Everything is all right now. Miranda can lie in the sun and soon she'll be dry.

Alice smiled down at the earnest little face. "Yes, poppet. Of course she will."

Poppy laid the doll down on the rug and ran off with Tom.

Julian put a hand on her shoulder. "Alice, whatever is the matter? You look ashen."

"Too much sun, I expect. I think I should go and lie down.

Alice left the children with Julian and went back to the house alone. She didn't know what drew her to the green bedroom, nor how she got there. As she sat down on the window seat she was still immersed in the scene she had witnessed at the lake. She relived those moments over and over again, feeling such an empathy with the mother of those children that she shared her grief as though it were her own.

It was the sight of Tom and Poppy staring at her from the doorway that returned her to the present reality. "Julian sent us to find you," said Poppy. "When you weren't in your room I thought you'd be here."

Chapter 13

Those summer weeks with the children were a bubble in time and Alice had become so accustomed to their company that it was a jolt to realise that her role in their lives would soon be over. It was one evening while they were having supper on the terrace that Julian reminded her.

"Felicity will be back in a weeks' time. She telephoned today and told me how much she's missed them," he said. "I doubt she'll be going on tour again, at least not in the near future."

They had just finished their meal and Tom ran off to play on the new space game that his mother had sent. Alice nodded and got up to clear the dishes.

"Miranda and I haven't finished yet, Alice," Poppy said, offering a spoonful of ice cream to the doll before it disappeared into her own mouth.

Alice smiled and sat down again. The day had been very warm and the evening air was sultry. She thought of how hot it must feel in London.

"Poor old Kate up in the smog," she said.

"Kate will be fine. They've got very effective air conditioning in the hotel," said Julian. He looked up at the sky. "There's a thunderstorm on the way. That should clear the air."

Poppy was communing with the doll as she scraped her dish clean. "Do you understand what she's saying?" he asked me.

"I'm afraid not," Alice said, laughing. "It's a language of her own devising."

Poppy got up from the table. "It's time for Miranda to go to bed."

"Right, sweetheart, off you go then," said Alice.

As she watched Poppy run off she thought how fortunate Felicity was to have such an enchanting daughter.

"You've grown very attached to her, haven't you?" Julian said, as though reading her mind.

"Yes. I love them both."

"Well, you don't have to lose touch, do you?"

"No, I hope not."

"Anyway, what about you? What are your plans?"

"I've told Kate that I'll stay on here for as long as she needs me. I don't plan to get another job until I've found somewhere to live."

Julian had intended to extricate himself from Kate and leave on Felicity's return. From the outset, he had never considered that their relationship was leading anywhere and hoped that by now she would have come to the same conclusion and ended it herself. Should he take the initiative Kate would want him out of the house. He wanted to leave, but not without Alice. In the present circumstances there was no way he could make his feelings for Alice known to her. His intuition told him that she, too, felt the chemistry between them but Alice was Kate's loyal friend. The predicament gnawed away at him.

"Well, I may stay on a while, too," he said casually. "Get in a few more rounds on that golf course."

"I thought you'd be taking the children back to London with you."

"I offered but Felicity wants to collect them. She wants to meet you."

"Oh?"

"Of course. Wouldn't you want to meet the person who has taken care of your kids the whole summer?"

"How is she?"

"I believe she's come to accept a life without Tim. She hasn't once mentioned him on the telephone."

"It can't have been easy for her."

"No, it wasn't." He chuckled to himself. "Mind you, Felicity turned into a veritable virago when she found out about Tim's affair but she never believed he would actually leave her. That was one hell of a shock."

"For you, too, I imagine."

"Not entirely. Theirs was always a tempestuous relationship. I could see the writing on the wall."

"Sounds like you were the one left to step in?"

"Seems that's what big brothers are for," he said with a chuckle. "Actually Tim came to stay with me when Felicity threw him out and he told me of his intention to leave the country. Naturally I did my best to dissuade him for the children's sake, but he wanted to make what he called a total break. That meant a separation of a few thousand miles between Felicity and himself."

The attic rooms were oppressively warm and it was a while before the children settled down. Once they were finally asleep Alice went down the back stairs to refill the water jug. The light was on in the kitchen and Julian was standing at the sink removing ice cubes from a tray.

He turned around and stared at her. "Oh, it's you, Alice!"

"I've come to get some water." said Alice.

"And I'm making iced tea," he said, scooping the ice into a jug. "Would you like some?"

She sat down on the Windsor chair and watched him stir the jug. "You gave me quite a start there," he said. He stared across at her and grinned. She was wearing an over-sized white t-shirt and bare feet. "Now I see why I mistook you for a ghostly apparition."

She pulled down the t-shirt over her knees. "Are you afraid of ghosts then, Julian?"

"Only the ones who creep up on me silently," he said and handed her a glass of the iced tea. He pulled up a chair and sat down opposite.

"What about you?"

"Afraid of ghosts? Well, I didn't give much thought to the afterlife until I came to this house. Now I seem to think of little else."

"Did you know that one of Ben's workmates spent a night camping in the house? He swore the house was haunted and moved into a B&B very fast."

"He was right. Have you heard the story of the children who drowned in the lake?"

He nodded.

"It's the spirit of their mother Eleanor he would have been aware of as I have myself. Poppy has seen her, too."

He looked taken aback. "Poppy?"

"Yes. She saw this woman by the lake and from what she described to me, it was no mortal."

"How did Poppy react?"

"As though it was perfectly natural. She wasn't bothered by it at all. Had she been upset I would have worried. It seemed best not to make an issue of it."

"I'm sure you're right. They do say that young children are innately psychic."

"Kate is very dismissive of the psychic world."

"That's not surprising. Kate is a pragmatist."

"Yes. She consulted a guest at the Manville about my hallucinations. He's a neurosurgeon from New York."

"What!"

"Kate was extremely well informed. She told me how an injury to this area of the skull can cause a brain malfunction," said Alice, pointing to a spot on the back on her head. "You see, she thought I'd hit my head on one of those beams in the attic and probably suffered a mild concussion."

"And did you?"

"Absolutely not. But it took some persuasion to convince her."

Julian roared with laughter. At the time Alice was annoyed by Kate's presumption but in retrospect she too found it funny.

"Next she called in a pest control company to get rid of whatever rodents were causing the disturbance in the attic."

Julian was still chuckling and Alice felt a twinge of disloyalty. "I don't blame Kate. Like most people, she sees the world as an orderly place over which we have total control. Once I thought so, too."

"What happens in this world isn't always rational. It's fear that makes us so sceptical."

"It may seem odd, but my gut feeling is that I've been singled out for a reason."

"I doubt that. Life can be very random."

For some while the sky had been rumbling ominously and suddenly a huge thunder clap rent the air. Julian got up and went to look out of the window. Rain started lashing against the window panes.

"I'd better go and check on Tom and Poppy," said Alice.

Julian gestured to her to stay put and headed for the back staircase. He stopped at the doorway and turned to her. "Not much point in going to bed yet. We won't get much sleep until it's over."

When he returned he reported that the children were fast asleep. The storm didn't die down for almost two hours and as they sat there sipping their tea she told him about Eleanor. He didn't react as though she were some kind of freak talking gibberish and it was a tonic for Alice to confide in someone with such an open mind.

"Thank you, Julian. Thank you for listening," she said before turning to go back up to bed.

"I think you're very brave, sweetheart," he said gently, taking her hand and brushing it with his lips. "Please talk to me whenever you want to."

Alice fell asleep quickly, but within what seemed like minutes she was woken by the sound of crying again. This time she knew it wasn't Poppy. She sat up in bed with her arms clasped tightly around her knees and listened to the muffled sobs until they subsided and died away. Afterwards she crept out of bed and opened the bedroom door. At the tower door she glimpsed a shadowy movement. She wanted to call out but no words would come.

The rain continued to fall heavily throughout the next morning but by mid-afternoon, just as Kate arrived, it suddenly ceased and an orange sun blazed in the clear blue sky. The rain on the motorway had slowed the traffic to gridlock and had added an extra hour to her journey, Kate complained.

"I am ready for a glass of wine," she said. "Let's go into the sitting room and catch up."

"Apart from the arrival of the cleaners this morning, there's not been much going on here," said Alice, sitting down in one of the comfy armchairs. "I kept the kids busy making chocolate cupcakes this morning. Poppy's turned out rather well but, much to Tom's dismay, his were rather a disaster."

Kate took a sip from her wine glass and leaned back on the sofa. "Remember that dinner party when our lemon soufflé disintegrated into a mousse and our clients demanded a discount, despite the fact that they ate the lot!"

Alice laughed. "And what about that time we left the chocolate sauce for the pear desert on the sideboard and that guy Gerald poured it all over your beautiful Beef Wellington!"

"Fortunately, I'd directed his guests towards the gravy boat but Gerald was too drunk to notice. He told me how delicious it was," Kate chuckled. "I'll never forget how he gave us that enormous tip at the end of the evening and you were too embarrassed to accept it."

"But you weren't. We spent our ill-gotten gains on very expensive hairdos at Robert Fielding!" said Alice.

"Oh, yes, so we did," said Kate.

They were giggling like a couple of schoolgirls and didn't notice Julian standing in the doorway. "Is this a private party?"

"Oh, come on in, Julian," said Kate, getting up. She poured him a glass of wine and filled up her own. "We were just reminiscing about our careers in the catering business."

"They were actually days of pure hedonism," said Alice. "So long as we made enough money to pay the rent, we really weren't bothered about anything but partying."

"And if you hadn't left me to go to St Martin's we might well have turned that little business into something big," said Kate.

"That's not fair, Kate. You could have found a replacement," said Alice.

"No, you're right. I was ready to move on, too," said Kate.

Julian turned to Alice in surprise. "You went to art college, Alice?"

Alice nodded. "I'm afraid I chucked it in. I left after eighteen months."

"And all because you moved in with the blue-eyed boy at the Beeb who didn't want his posh friends to know he was living with a student," said Kate.

"No, Kate. That's not true. It was my decision. I wanted to get a job," said Alice.

"But Richard was earning enough money, wasn't he?

"I wanted to be independent."

"Well I can't tell you how envious I was of your lifestyle in those days. I was at the bottom of the ladder earning a pittance and there were you, swanning around with that glamorous crowd and having such interesting media types to dinner."

Alice laughed. "Oh, Kate. You must have seen my life through rose-tinted spectacles. I was never a part of that crowd. If you weren't in the media yourself, you might as well have been invisible."

"Perhaps you were just too young and green to know how to handle it," said Kate, kindly. "I know what I'd have done with the tossers!"

Julian grinned. "I think we can well imagine."

Kate snorted at him. "Well, Ali, you've now got the chance to take up your art again. So grab it!"

Julian drank up his wine and put down the glass. "Why don't we go and look at the sunset. It's going to be rather special tonight."

"Yes, you go ahead. I'll join you in a bit. First I must make a phone call," said Kate.

"We'll get the best vantage point here," said Julian, walking with Alice to the bench at the top of the west lawn.

The house was situated above a valley with only a barrier of fir trees to protect it from the mercy of the elements. The advantage of its exalted position was that it offered unsurpassed views of the surrounding countryside. Splashed across the horizon were vibrant shades of pinks and mauves merging into crimson fringed in bright orange.

For a while they sat in silence, Julian sitting about a foot away from her with his arm stretched out along the back of the bench. He was wearing a t-shirt and when he shifted his position Alice could feel the hair on his arm brushing against the skin on her neck. This intimate physical contact aroused her and she shivered. Gradually, over the weeks, Alice had become increasingly and uncomfortably aware of her attraction to him but nothing so intense had happened before. She edged away along the bench.

He glanced at her sideways and saw how vulnerable she looked. He ached to put his arm around her and hold her close. Instead, he reached out his hand and tucked back a strand of hair that had fallen across her face. As he bent towards her, his face almost brushed against hers. She was maddened to feel her face flush.

"Tell me, Alice, have you always felt like the outsider?"

"Hmm, I suppose I have. I'm probably too introspective. Oh dear, I must sound like a lost cause!"

He smiled. Her self-deprecation was very endearing and he marvelled, not for the first time, at how she stirred emotions that he hadn't expected to feel again.

"On the contrary I think you're just true to yourself," he said. "It's a very attractive quality."

Kate was walking towards them and she had a spring in her step. "Well, I've just finalised the deal with the TV lawyers. It's all set for October," she said, sitting down between them.

"That's marvellous news, Kate," said Alice. "Well done!"

Kate smiled with satisfaction. "To have the hotel featured on TV will be great PR." She put a hand on Alice's arm. "Ali, why don't you think about coming into the business? I could do with someone like you on the team."

"Just a moment ago you were urging me to pursue my art!" said Alice with a grin.

"Yes. You can do that, too," said Kate.

"To be honest Kate, I don't think I'd be suited to the hotel business," said Alice.

Julian winked at her. "Kate would have us all on board, if she could."

She shot him a quelling glance. "I have more discernment than you realise, Julian."

"I can see it now, Alice running this place whilst your management skills are spread far and wide," he said.

Kate ignored him and turned to Alice. "By the way, that American girl Erin phoned. She wanted to talk to you and said she'd call back in the morning."

"Oh, I remember Erin. What an enchanting young woman!" said Julian, his eyes lighting up mischievously. "Is she paying us a return visit?"

"No, she isn't." said Kate. "Erin is back in the United States."

"For a moment you raised my hopes," he said.

"Do shut up, Julian," said Kate. "The girl's half your age."

Their familiar banter restored Alice's equilibrium, at least for the time being.

The following day Alice was in the office showing Suzie how Kate liked the menus printed when Erin phoned.

"Like you told me, you were working when you came to the US last time, now is the chance for you to see the other side. Come and have some fun!" she said down the line.

Kate came into the room. "How are you doing here?" she asked Suzie.

Suzie looked up brightly. "The menus, Kate. All done and dusted. I can manage this in future."

"Excellent," said Kate, taking the menus out of the printer tray and handing them to her. "I'd like you to take them to Victor, please."

"That was Erin," said Alice, replacing the receiver. "She was ringing to remind me of Art's invitation to Florida."

"Where in Florida does he live?"

"It's a place called Naples."

"Very nice, too. Naples is a pretty exclusive area," said Kate. "Will you go?"

"I haven't decided. Would you mind if I did?"

"Why should I mind? The guests will be gone by mid-September."

"My priority is to find a flat so I should start looking, not going off on holiday."

"Do you have an area in mind?"

"Probably South London. I've got used to it there."

"Well, let me talk to Ben. He's based in Clapham and gets to hear about most of the properties before they come on the market."

Alice followed Kate out into the kitchen. "Just the table arrangements to do now," said Kate, gathering a handful of flowers from a bucket and spreading them across the sideboard. "Suzie asked me why I don't get in the florists, but this is a job I really enjoy. It's different in London. Here we have all these wonderful flowers, even now so late in the summer."

"This is my favourite," said Alice, picking up a blue delphinium. "Someone's put a lot of love into this garden."

"Yes, Ellen Henshaw is a very keen horticulturist."

"Dave told me she lives in the village now."

"That's right. She's got a pretty little cottage on the green," said Kate. "That reminds me, I really need to speak to her. I found an old leather trunk in the cellar that must belong to her. God knows how it got overlooked in the move."

"Maybe I could drop it over to her. I'd like to meet Miss Henshaw."

"Right. I'll give her a bell."

The last week of the hotel's summer season seemed to pass in a flash and the day after the last guests' departure it was time for Tom and Poppy to leave. Alice had arranged to meet Ben that afternoon and was upstairs packing up the remains of the children's toys when Felicity arrived.

It was an emotional day and Alice wanted to leave without any fuss, but as she hovered outside the sitting room considering this option, Kate caught sight of her. "Ah, there you are, Ali. Come and meet Felicity," she said and beckoned her in.

A petite dark-haired woman got up from her chair and walked across to Alice. She was dressed with the kind of casual elegance that is costly to acquire. "So you must be Alice," she said, shaking her hand. "I've heard so much about you from Julian, but he didn't tell me how pretty you were!" Her voice was a soft, husky drawl.

"Alice, Alice," Poppy called out. "Look what Mummy's got me!"

The children were sitting on the floor ripping the paper from a variety of packages and Alice went over to admire Poppy's golden-haired doll. "Look, Alice, she wees and she can talk!"

Felicity picked up a parcel from the table and handed it to Alice. "Here's a little something for you, my dear," she said.

Alice took the parcel and went to sit on the sofa next to Kate. Under the pretty wrapping was a large cashmere shawl. It was woven in shades of pale aquamarine merging into azure blue that resembled the sky on a mid-summer's day.

"Oh, isn't it gorgeous!" said Kate, draping it over Alice's shoulders. "It feels like gossamer."

"And what beautiful colours. Thank you, Felicity," said Alice.

Felicity turned to Julian. "How clever of you, darling. You said she'd like blue!"

"What I said is that blue suits Alice," he said.

Alice raised her eyebrows and shot him a quizzical glance. He winked back at her.

"I believe I have a lot to thank you for, Alice. Julian's told me what a gem you've been," said Felicity. "He says you've transformed two spoiled little brats into civilised human beings!"

Whilst she was relating risqué anecdotes about the sexual activities of various cast members, in particular her gay leading man, Alice studied her more closely, observing the expressive hazel eyes and sharply chiselled features. Poppy had inherited her mother's eyes and colouring though Poppy's face was more oval and much softer. Felicity's looks were attractive rather than beautiful, but she had the type of presence that would turn men's heads in any gathering.

Alice had not been looking forward to this day and still hoped to slip away unnoticed. She glanced at Tom and Poppy. They were happily engrossed in their new toys and it seemed like an opportune moment to make a discreet exist. "I'm afraid I've got to go," she whispered to Kate.

"Can't you stay and have some lunch?" Kate asked.

"No, I've promised to meet Ben at 3.30. He's got some properties to show me," she said.

Kate followed her out to the car. "Well, what did you think of her?" she asked.

"A bit condescending."

"Yes, she can be a patronising bitch," Kate chuckled. "And don't be fooled by those taut features, they owe more to the surgeon's knife than nature."

"How old is she then?"

"According to her publicists she's thirty-five though I happen to know she was forty four last birthday," Kate said with a satisfied grin.

"Well, she does look good, though so slight and fragile you'd think a gust of wind would blow her over," said Alice.

"Don't you believe it!" Kate said in exclamation. "Felicity's as tough and as shrewd as they come."

"Not clever enough to hold on to her husband though, was she?" said Alice.

"No. But now I see she has other plans, like getting her talons into his older brother."

"I doubt Julian would play ball."

Kate laughed. "I'd challenge any woman to try it!"

Alice sat behind the wheel of the car and was about to turn on the ignition when Poppy came bounding out into the driveway.

Alice got out of the car and Poppy clasped her arms around Alice's neck. "I'm going to miss you lots, Alice."

"Me, too, sweetheart," said Alice, hugging her tightly.

Chapter 14

"It would be a great investment, Ali," said Ben, inserting a key in the front door lock. "Like I said, it's not even on the market yet. I only heard about it three days ago."

Alice was expecting to view flats, but Ben had insisted they take a look at this end of terrace house near the centre of Clapham.

On the ground floor there were two reception rooms and a good sized kitchen, but the house was in a bad state of repair.

Alice stared doubtfully at the huge patch of damp on the sitting room wall. "It needs a lot of work."

Ben glanced at the wall and went upstairs. She followed him into the bathroom. "There's a leak from the shower fitting, nothing major," he said.

The lavatory and the bathroom were separate and their old-fashioned fittings were chipped, stained or broken. "Look, what I suggest is that we knock down this wall and you'll get a really good sized bathroom," he said.

Alice glanced around the shabby kitchen with its 1950s green-tiled walls. "We'll have to update this of course," said Ben, running his hand across the stained Formica tops. "I haven't checked the wiring yet, but apart from a new kitchen and bathroom suite, the work's mostly cosmetic."

He saw her hesitation. "It's a very sound property and in pretty good nick considering that students have been living here. I'd buy it myself if I had the money."

"It's a bit over my budget, Ben."

"Put in an offer. I heard the vendor's in a hurry to sell."

Alice took another look at the reception room at the back of the house. Through the French windows was a small, neglected garden. When she went outside to investigate she discovered beneath the undergrowth a pretty brick path leading down to a sundial at the bottom of the garden. She pictured an archway of roses sprawled over it.

Ben came up behind her. "We could go and see the flat now, if you like."

She turned around and smiled at him. "No need."

Alice spent that night at the hotel with Kate and first thing the following morning she put in a bid with the vendor's solicitors. When she arrived back at Langsmead there was a telephone message from Miss Henshaw inviting her to tea that afternoon. She went to find Dave in the garden and asked him to cut some flowers for her. He knew Miss Henshaw's favourites and went from border to border, snipping off a variety of beautiful blooms.

At one end of the picturesque village green there was a 300-year-old stone well and Alice was informed by Dave that it used to supply water for the entire local community. After hauling the trunk into the back of her car he had suggested he should accompany her to offload it at the cottage.

Opposite the well was the cricket pitch and pavilion, a unique wooden structure that had been erected during the first year of Queen Victoria's reign. It was the perfect setting for Miss Henshaw's picture-book cottage.

She stood waiting for them at the front door and ushered Alice in with a welcoming smile. Miss Henshaw was around seventy and had the kind of appearance that typified a spinster of her generation and class living in rural England at that time. Her grey hair was neatly permed and she wore a twinset with a shapeless tweed skirt and sturdy leather shoes.

After depositing the trunk into a back room, Dave declined the tea Miss Henshaw offered and walked off down the road. Meanwhile, Alice was led into a cosy sitting room and directed to an armchair. Miss Henshaw disappeared into the kitchen with the flowers. When she reappeared she carried a tray of tea and scones and they chatted about her move into the village.

"I thought I would miss the old place, but to tell you the truth, it was only the garden I was sad to leave. It's really rather nice to live in the hub of things here without having to worry how the bills will get paid."

While she was in the kitchen Alice's eye had roved around the sitting room and rested on the silver framed photograph that took pride of place on the mantlepiece. It was a formal black and white photograph of a good-looking man of about thirty. He was dressed in the uniform of an RAF officer and sported a neat moustache.

"Is that young man a member of your family?" asked Alice when Miss Henshaw returned to the room.

"Oh, no. That's Anthony, my fiancé."

She went across to the mantlepiece and picked up the photograph. "He was a squadron leader," she said proudly. "While I was reading the newspaper this morning I realised it was the anniversary of the day we got engaged. That was in '38, but then the war came and our wedding was postponed."

She handed Alice the photograph. "He's very handsome," said Alice.

"Yes, he was," she said with a sigh. "He was killed in a bombing raid over Berlin. Only three of his squadron returned."

Alice handed back the photograph and Miss Henshaw returned it to its place on the mantlepiece and went to sit down.

"My brother Michael was luckier than most. He lost a leg but he did survive. When Michael came home at the end of the war he came back to the house and lived with me after our parents died."

Alice watched her pouring the tea from a silver tea pot. "Were you born at Langsmead Hall, Miss Henshaw?" she asked.

"Oh, no. When my father inherited the property I was about four or five," she said. "My uncle Henry was on board the Lusitania, you see. He was on his return from America when the ship went down."

"So your uncle had no heirs of his own?" said Alice.

Miss Henshaw shook her head. "None living. His two young children drowned in the lake."

"Yes. Dave told me. What an awful tragedy."

"Yes," said Miss Henshaw, putting down her teacup. "There was a dangerous undertow by the bridge, you see. It sucked them under. Afterwards that end of the lake was blocked off. And what a dark, gloomy place it was. When my brother and I were young, we believed that evil spirits lurked there, it was certainly very eerie."

"Did you know their mother?" asked Alice.

"Ah, you're referring to Uncle Henry's widow Eleanor. I may have met her, but I was too young to remember. She died before we moved into the house."

"Did you ever suspect that the house was haunted, Miss Henshaw?" asked Alice.

"Yes. I most definitely did." She paused for a moment. "There is a very troubled spirit in that house. I never liked living there alone. After my brother died, I always made sure that the housekeeper was within earshot."

"I have very good reason to believe that spirit to be Eleanor, your uncle's widow."

"Hmm. That comes as no surprise to me, Miss Ainsley. I don't know how you have come to that conclusion, but I wouldn't doubt it for one moment."

She offered Alice another of her freshly baked scones. "When I was a girl, no one was allowed to mention Eleanor. It was as though they wanted to blot out all traces of her."

"Why would they do that?"

"It was a different age, my dear. There were different values," she said, wiping her hands on a linen napkin. "These days nobody would care, I dare say, but at that time it was considered shocking for a woman to take a lover and worse still to give birth to an illegitimate child."

"You mean Eleanor had a third child?"

"Oh, yes. A year or so after Henry's death," said Miss Henshaw. "You can't imagine the stigma for the family."

"What happened to Eleanor and her baby?" asked Alice.

"Apparently, neither of them survived. That was why my father inherited the estate. The servants were told that Eleanor died from a fever."

"You don't sound convinced?"

"That she died from a fever? No I'm not. About how or exactly when she died I have no idea. She wasn't buried in the family plot or anywhere else in the local cemetery. I made it my business to find out."

"What did you make of it?"

Miss Henshaw paused. "It remains a mystery to this day. You see, I would never have known about Eleanor had it not been for Aggie."

"Who is Aggie, Miss Henshaw?"

"Ah, yes. Dear Aggie," she said, putting down her tea cup. "Aggie was married to Dave's grandfather. At the age of fourteen she'd been plucked from a Catholic orphanage for girls by my aunt Maude. By all accounts, it was a harsh place though I don't imagine that working as personal maid to Maude was much better."

"So your aunt brought Aggie to Langsmead, did she?"

"Yes, Aggie would have been about seventeen then. She only knew Eleanor for a very brief time but Eleanor showed the girl great kindness. She never forgot that."

"What about the other servants, didn't they talk about Eleanor?"

"When my parents moved to Langsmead they brought their own servants with them, but Aggie married Dave's grandfather and moved into his cottage on the estate. She used to come over to the house to help with the cleaning."

Miss Henshaw glanced at her watch and Alice feared she had overstayed her welcome. "I'm sorry to have taken up so much of your time," she said.

"Oh, not at all, my dear. I've enjoyed talking to you. Now, however, I have a bridge game to attend."

"Thank you very much for sharing all this with me. It's been very interesting," said Alice, getting up.

Miss Henshaw walked with her out to the hallway. "I was always curious to uncover the mystery surrounding Eleanor for myself, but time passes and you come to realise that sometimes you must let things be."

After she arrived back at the house Alice went into the library to return the book she had just finished. She liked this room. The oak-panelled walls and Arts and Craft features lent it a masculine charm. She glanced at the large baize-covered table where Julian had instructed Tom on the rudiments of snooker and smiled at the memory. As she reached up to replace her book on the shelf, the light dimmed. She turned around, thinking it must be caused by a power surge, but the room was transformed by the yellow glow of gas lamps. Alice had company.

Henry sat in his favourite armchair by the fireplace and watched Eleanor pour the tea. He gazed at the graceful curve of her neck as she bent over the teacups and, as always, he was moved by his young wife's loveliness. Although he was perplexed by the unusual radiance he had noticed in recent months, he could not deny that it enhanced her allure.

Henry was reminded of a conversation that had taken place eleven years before when his elder sister Maude had questioned him about the wisdom of choosing such a young bride, but Henry had been besotted by Eleanor's beauty. He decided that her youth was to his advantage because he could mould her into exactly the wife that he required. Yet there was a mercurial quality in Eleanor that eluded him. It excited and disturbed him in equal measure.

A few years after their marriage and the birth of their two children, Henry had been offered a prestigious job in the civil service. This new position obliged him to spend the week in London, and although occasionally he required Eleanor to join him, he allowed her to live with the children at Langsmead, the country house he had inherited from his father. For Eleanor it was a miraculous reprieve from the conjugal demands of the bedroom. Henry was an uncouth lover. He was a highly sexed man whose libido had been satisfied by the services of the whores at the London brothels he frequented, and he was not attuned to the sensibilities of an educated, cultured young woman.

Henry had to admit that, to her credit, Eleanor had fulfilled her wifely duties and produced two healthy babies within quick succession As a hostess at his table he could not fault her and when his contemporaries complimented him on his enchanting young wife, he relished their envy. Yet what Henry secretly craved was the kind of affection that he saw her lavishing upon the children, but however much he indulged her, it was denied him. Equally infuriating to him was the amount of time she squandered on her cousins. He blamed Eleanor's exuberant and demonstrative nature on her father's Irish blood, though he wouldn't have minded it so acutely had her attitude to him been less reserved.

"I think that you spend too much time with your cousins," said Henry.

Following the death of Eleanor's mother, Henry had grudgingly accepted his wife's desire for the company of Martha and Jonathan, the cousins with whom she had spent much of her youth.

Eleanor glanced across at him. "Why, Henry? You've never objected before."

"Because your place is here, and I don't think they are a good influence."

Eleanor raised her eyebrows indignantly. "But I only visit them occasionally, no more than four or five times a year."

"God's teeth, woman! You spent a week with them only two months ago, and each time you go there you come back with your head stuffed full with their radical ideas."

"What radical ideas are you referring to, Henry?" she asked, coldly.

"Isn't your cousin Martha a suffragette?"

"No, Henry. Martha is sympathetic to the cause. She may be liberated in her thinking, but she is also a very responsible person."

"And why should women need to vote, anyway?" asked Henry. "Isn't it their place to support their husbands and take care of their children?"

"That has nothing to do with their unequal status," she said, evenly.

"Poppycock! It seems I have allowed you too much freedom. That must be curtailed."

Eleanor looked at Henry indignantly. "I don't believe I fail in my duties as a wife and mother. In fact, I'm surprised you want to deny me the little time I spend with Martha and Jonathan."

"The point is that you should empty your head of Martha's radical notions. Asquith's party will never give women the vote, nor will any other right-minded government," Henry said.

"In fact, Henry, Jonathan has just joined his regiment in France, and Martha is too busy with her nurse's training to have time for anything else."

Eleanor had been concerned that Henry might have heard rumours about her meetings with Declan. He was a close friend to Jonathan and six months previously he and Eleanor had been reunited at a dinner party in her cousins' home. Declan was now a heart surgeon at a London hospital. He had not married and his love for Eleanor was unchanged.

Eleanor could see that Henry was in a dangerous mood, and feared that next he would be reminding her of the debt that she owed him. She knew she was behaving recklessly and sometimes these days she felt her emotions running wild; one moment she thanked God that her lover's career had so far kept him out of the war but then flew into a panic about the dangerous game she was playing. Her relief was immense when she discovered that Henry had other things on his mind.

"I have something of importance to tell you, Eleanor." he said. He cleared his throat before continuing. "I will shortly be taking part in a war mission and this will entail a visit to the United States of America."

"You're going to America?"

"Yes, Eleanor. This war is now in its seventh month and with still no end in sight. We need the Americans with us. I am therefore to be part of a delegation representing the War Office. My mission involves negotiations between the American government and our own."

Eleanor glanced at him in surprise. Henry had never before discussed anything connected with his official work.

"Due to this enforced absence, I have decided it best that George should go away to school without delay. I have made arrangements accordingly," he said.

Eleanor stared at him, aghast. "But Henry, you can't do that! You promised that you wouldn't send him away for at least another year. He hasn't yet had his tenth birthday!"

"I don't believe it is in George's best interests to leave him in a household that lacks sufficient discipline for a growing boy."

"No, Henry. He's too young. He's still a baby!"

"Exactly my point and I should remind you that normally boys go away to school at seven or eight, as I did myself. It's time for George to learn how to become a man."

"No Henry. Please," she said, imploringly.

"That is my final word on the matter. We will speak no more of it."

At that moment Eleanor felt nothing but intense dislike for her husband, but in view of his obduracy, she knew her best strategy was to placate him.

"We'll be sorry to see you go," she said, feigning a sympathetic smile. "When will you be leaving us?"

"I shall be embarking at Liverpool in two weeks' time and sailing on the Lusitania. Although officially requisitioned for war duties, at present the vessel continues her transatlantic passenger services."

Due to Henry's imminent departure, Eleanor knew she had time on her side and her fears for George abated. She could now afford to be generous.

"It's terrible that this accursed war should be taking you away, Henry. But I do, of course, realise that you must do your duty, as always."

Henry nodded, satisfied by her compliant mood. At that moment he decided that another pregnancy would retain his wife's docility and he would instruct his sister Maude to keep an eye on the household during his absence.

"I shall ask Maude to keep you company," he said.

Eleanor had made no secret of her dislike of Henry's overbearing elder sister and she could no longer accept

Henry's patronising attitude. Her eyes flashed in anger. "That won't be necessary, Henry. I can run my own household!"

Later, as Alice came out of the library, Julian opened the study door and saw her walking across the hall towards the kitchen. "Alice," he called.

She turned in surprise. "Oh, hello, Julian."

"Is everything all right? You look distracted."

"Yes. It's just..."

"What?"

She was about to tell him what she had witnessed in the library but changed her mind. "You startled me. That's all. I didn't know you were here."

"I've been in the study for most of the day, going over the proofs."

"I didn't see your car."

"No, it's up at the garage having some repairs done."

"Oh, I see."

"Dave told me you had gone to visit Ellen Henshaw."

"Yes. What I discovered is extraordinary."

"Oh, playing sleuth now, are we?"

Alice nodded. "Miss Henshaw is a mine of information."

Maria was in the kitchen preparing their supper when she should have been off duty. "You can leave that to me, Maria," Alice told her. "Kate's not back until tomorrow. Why don't you take the evening off?"

Since those intimate moments whilst watching the sunset, Alice hadn't spent any time alone with Julian and was nervous of doing so. She scoured the *TV Times* and found a film that might be worth watching and when she told him how she intended to spend the evening, he suggested they take their supper into the sitting room.

"I'll make up the fire," he said. "The evenings are getting chilly."

The film turned out to be an engrossing murder mystery that kept them riveted to the screen for two hours. When the end credits started to roll, Alice got up and started to clear up the coffee table.

"I've got a theory about your ghost," he said.

"Oh?"

"It came to me while we were watching the film," he said, flicking the off button on the remote control.

He took the tray of empty dishes from her and carried it out to the kitchen. A few minutes later he returned and threw another log on the fire.

"It's about that doll you unearthed in the attic, the doll that Poppy was so attached to," he said.

"She left it behind, you know," said Alice. "I was surprised."

"It could be a malevolent force."

She stared at him. "What? Are you suggesting that the doll is some kind of ghoul?"

He sat down on the sofa beside her. "Have you ever heard of a jinn?"

"No."

"In Muslim demonology there's a spirit called a jinn that has the power to exercise a supernatural influence over people."

"I'm not sure I understand."

"What I'm saying is that the doll could be the catalyst."

"Quite possible," she said, recalling that enigmatic expression as it lay on Poppy's pillow.

"Did Poppy give you a reason for not taking the doll with her?"

"She said that it belonged here. She was very clear about that."

"Oh, what a fey child!"

Alice told him what she had learned about Eleanor from Miss Henshaw and how strange it was that there was no headstone for her in the village cemetery.

"There could be a simple explanation for that."

"Like what?"

"Eleanor may have left and gone to live with her lover."

"Not according to Agnes, the maid. She was there at the time."

"The other possibility is suicide. If that was the case, burial in consecrated ground would not have been permitted."

"I don't believe it was that. I think she was murdered."

"Murdered? But there would have been a police enquiry and the servants would have known about that."

"Not necessarily. Not if it was kept secret."

"You should put all this out of your mind, Alice."

She stared into the flames of the fire and shook her head. She had to uncover the mystery. "It's too late for that."

"Look, Alice, this woman Eleanor is becoming an obsession. Obsessions are dangerous. I think you should take a leaf out of Miss Henshaw's book and let sleeping dogs lie."

When she got up to leave, he caught hold of her hand. "I have a healthy respect for the occult and that is why I don't like the idea of you getting so involved. You're too vulnerable."

"I can handle it."

He got up, still holding on to her hand. "I'm only speaking like this because I care about you, Alice. I care a great deal."

The feeling between them was powerful but she pulled her hand away, resisting her desire to feel his arms around her. He held her eyes and the look that they exchanged was charged with a myriad emotions.

Chapter 15

It was a relief to find that Julian was already in his study when Alice came downstairs the next morning. She could not remain in such close proximity to him any longer. It was time for her to leave the house. She would tell Kate over lunch and with the decision made she felt a great deal better.

While Alice was de-boning the fish for a kedgeree she received a phone call about the Clapham house. It was the vendor's solicitor to tell her that her offer had been accepted.

Alice was bursting with excitement when Kate walked in through the back door.

"Wow! You got it!" Kate exclaimed, dropping a parcel on the table. "No haggling about the price?"

"No. The vendor needed a cash offer. His company are moving him abroad."

"Lucky girl!" said Kate and gave her a hug.

Alice bustled about the kitchen. "Yes. I can hardly believe it! Sit down, Kate. I'll make us coffee."

"Hmm, something smells good!"

"Oh, the kedgeree!" Alice hurried over to the pan on the Aga. "I'll have to give Maxie a ring. They want completion within six weeks!"

"You don't mean Maxine Barker?"

Maxine had been a law student during their flat-sharing days and sometimes she had helped out with the catering business.

"Yes. Maxie is doing the conveyancing," said Alice, stirring rice into the pan of smoked haddock and bacon.

"I thought Maxie was a hausfrau. She was living out in the sticks last time I saw her. Remember that ghastly barbecue at the marital home and those babies that never stopped screaming? I couldn't understand how such a bright girl like Maxie could have got herself so lumbered!"

"I was rather envious," said Alice.

"Ali, you can't be serious!"

"Yes. She looked so happy."

"Good God! Did she really?"

Alice poured the coffee and put down a mug on the table for Kate. "You know, Maxie has been working for a firm of solicitors in Richmond for the last two years. She dealt with my sale of the Twickenham house."

"Oh, so she came to her senses, did she? Has she dumped that dreary husband as well?"

"No, Kate. She's still married to Ken and the screaming babies are now at primary school, by the way."

Kate sat down. "Well, well. I guess it takes all kinds." She lit a cigarette and took a long drag. "Take us for instance. We have such different expectations of life we're chalk and cheese, but we still seem to rub along pretty well. And best of all we've never clashed over men! In fact, Ali, you are the best friend I've ever had. It's been so good to have you around."

Alice felt a pall of shame as she put the salad bowl on the table. She looked across at Kate. "And I've had a wonderful summer here, Kate, but now it's time for me to go."

"But you won't have the house for weeks and then you'll have builders moving in. There's no need for you to rush off yet."

Alice wished she could tell Kate why her departure couldn't wait. "I really should."

"That's nonsense. Unless you tell me you have a secret assignation with a lover I really won't hear of it!"

Alice went back to the stove and as she sprinkled coriander over the kedgeree, she decided to accept the invitation to Florida.

"Sometimes, you know, Ali, I wish I could be more like you," said Kate.

Alice spooned the kedgeree into an earthenware dish and laughed. "What on earth do you mean?"

"You're not driven like I am."

Alice turned around and stared at her. "But look at what you have achieved, Kate!"

Kate grimaced. "A semi-basement flat in Maida Vale that I hardly ever see and a whacking great mortgage."

Alice shook her head. "A board of directors you have eating out of your hand and a personality that people don't forget. You and the Manville are synonymous."

"To tell you the truth it's been great to be back. The challenge of getting this place up and running has been terrific, but I need the buzz of a big city. I've missed that."

"That's not surprising. You're a city girl."

"Yes. It's where I'm supposed to be."

Alice moved Kate's package in order to lay the table. "Oh for goodness sake, I almost forgot! That's for you," said Kate.

Underneath the brown paper wrapping was a wooden easel, a set of canvases and oil paints and a full complement of accessories.

"It's to say thank you for all your support," said Kate.

Alice was thrilled. "Oh, thank you, Kate. It feels like Christmas!"

Julian joined them for lunch around the kitchen table. Alice managed to avoid any eye contact which wasn't too difficult because Kate was in a bubbly mood and chattered on about the interesting people she was meeting.

"I'm getting invitations to A-list parties so I must be doing something right!" she said with a chuckle.

Julian smiled indulgently. "You really like rubbing shoulders with celebrities, don't you Kate?"

"Of course I do. It's the most fun part of the job," she said.

"And you are the draw that brings them to the Manville so that makes you a celebrity in your own right," said Alice.

Kate flashed Alice a smile. "By the way, Julian, the Hollywood producer Judd Evans is staying at the moment and he told me how much he'd like to meet you. I told him I'd arrange it."

"Why does he want to meet me?" said Julian.

"Because he loves your novels. He thinks *The Lion's Den* would make a great movie and he'd like to buy the film rights. I said we could meet up next week."

"He'd best talk to my agent," said Julian.

"Well that fell a bit flat!" said Kate. "Wouldn't you like to see your novel turned into a film?"

"Thank you, Kate. It's good of you to think of me. The thing is people often want to buy film rights and some of them do, maybe even get a screenplay written but whether it actually gets turned into a film doesn't necessarily follow. It is the agent who negotiates these deals."

Kate shrugged. She turned to Alice and asked whether she remembered two elderly English women who stayed at Langsmead the first week they opened.

"Yes, I do," said Alice. "Why do you ask?"

"It turns out that one of them is a psychic and highly esteemed in her field," said Kate.

"How do you know that?" Alice asked.

"Because Mrs Huntley recommended us to the psychic society and they want to hold a convention here," said Kate. "They also said something about an exorcism. Extraordinary how people imagine all old houses are haunted. You know, while she was staying here, Mrs Huntley warned me about a turbulence in the atmosphere."

"I wish I'd known. I'd like to have talked to her," said Alice.

"Well, I thought she was referring to the weather!" said Kate.

Alice laughed. "Oh, Kate!"

Julian got up, thanked them for the lunch and said he was going back to work. As he left, he stopped in the doorway. "Oh, Kate, by the way, I will be leaving on Monday."

Kate look up at him. "Oh?"

"I've got to spend next week with my editor," he said.

"Actually that works rather well. It will save you a trip."

"What trip?"

"A drive up to town to meet Judd," said Kate. "I promised we'd have dinner with him next week."

"Without consulting me first?"

"I assumed you'd want to."

"Sometimes one can presume too much," he said. "I'm not your lapdog, Kate."

Kate stared after him and tutted. "Why is he so bloody-minded? I was only trying to be helpful!"

"When are you going back to town, Kate?" asked Alice.

"As a matter of fact I've arranged to spend an extra couple of days here to catch up on the office work," she said.

"I thought I might shoot off first thing tomorrow," said Alice. "You see, I'm accepting the invitation to Florida and I need to buy a ticket.

"Couldn't that wait another day?"

That afternoon Alice took her new easel and paints down to the lake and set herself up on the embankment. Autumn beckoned and the bright sunshine accentuated the gold and copper foliage. She squeezed thick swirls of Prussic blue and Cameron yellow onto her palette, added more yellow and lots of white.

She didn't make a sketch and her first brush strokes were tentative, but emboldened by the landscape and the perfect light, the brush moved swiftly between palette and board. Colours were rapidly filling the white space as she layered the paint on in thick, broad strokes, then mixed more white to capture the more subtle hues. With her senses entirely in control, she hardly noticed the passage of time. Nor, even when the sun, moving slowly overhead, highlighted the shadowy image of a female figure, was she consciously aware of its intrusion onto the canvas.

She worked fast to finish before the light changed, but when she looked at the final result she was startled by the feminine image that had emerged through the green and gold landscape. She stared at it for a moment then added a few stokes to the outline of her pale turquoise gown and wide straw hat.

"This is brilliant!" Kate said as she pushed up a table against the wood panelled wall in the grand hall and propped the canvas on it. She stood back to appraise it. "It has such a dreamy feel, Ali. You've managed to capture that elusive moment just as the seasons change."

"And that ubiquitous ghost," said Julian, coming to stand beside Kate.

Alice glanced at him in surprise. It was Eleanor. Alice realised how deeply Eleanor was imbued in her subconscious. Her affinity with the dead woman was puzzling and often perplexing. She needed to know the reason.

"It really deserves to be up on the wall, not hidden away like most of your paintings," said Kate.

Alice had painted as though driven and had never painted in oil so fast. She was pleasantly surprised by its reception. "Would you like to have it, Kate?" she said. "I think it belongs here."

"Oh, yes please. I'd love to keep it," said Kate. "And I'll see that it gets properly framed." She gestured towards the formal portrait of a solemn Edwardian woman hanging on the wall of the first flight of stairs. "Look, wouldn't it look great up there?"

"Spirit of the Lake. That's what you could call it," said Julian.

"Yes, I like that. Perhaps you could paint others, Ali," said Kate. "I'm sure our guests would appreciate them.

We could even offer them for sale. A souvenir of their visit to this house."

Julian shook his head. "Oh, Kate, must you turn everything into a commercial venture?"

His tone to her lately was more irritable than Alice had heard him use before and judging by Kate's expression she didn't like it one bit. "It was just a thought. Ali needs encouragement. Why do you always have something so negative to say?"

By the following day the atmosphere in the house had become very strained and Alice was glad to escape outside with her sketch book. When she popped into the kitchen she found Maria at the sink staring disconsolately out of the window. Alice put a hand on her shoulder "Whatever is the matter, Maria?"

"It's Miss Kate. She snaps at me twice this morning. What I have done to displease her she doesn't say."

"Don't worry, Maria. I'm sure it's nothing personal. I expect she's got a lot on her mind."

Alice showed her the sketch she had drawn of the Gate House. Maria studied it and her face brightened.

"I could make a painting of it if you like," said Alice.

Maria gave a big smile. "A picture of my English house! Yes, I would like it very much."

It started to rain in the afternoon and Alice was forced to take shelter inside. Late in the afternoon, she was standing on the galleried landing about to go downstairs when she heard Kate's voice raised in anger and shortly afterwards the crunch of car tyres on the gravel driveway. Moments later Kate came striding up the stairs walking past Alice as though she was invisible. The telephone started to ring and she ran down the stairs to Kate's office.

Later, when she went up to find Kate, her bedroom door stood slightly ajar and she glimpsed Kate standing at the window, staring out at the rain.

Alice popped her head around the door. "Kate, there was someone on the phone called Peter Clarke. He has a query about tomorrow's convention. It sounded urgent."

Kate didn't turn around. "Oh, fuck it! I must have forgotten to put on the answering machine."

Alice went into the room. "Kate, are you okay?"

"Yes. I just want to be left alone. Is that so much to ask?"

Alice made a fast retreat.

The drawing room had been transformed into a conference hall for the delegates of a business consortium and was dominated by a huge mahogany table. Alice helped Victor to carry in the chairs and they had just finished arranging them around the table when Kate came into the room.

"I'd like to talk to you," she said, quietly.

Alice followed her into the sitting room. Kate closed the door behind them and went to sit down. "I'm sorry that I snapped at you earlier. I have called Peter back."

Alice nodded and sat down. "It's okay."

There was a knock on the door and Maria bustled in with a tray of tea and cake.

"Thank you, Maria," said Kate.

She looked at Kate quizzically. "Will Mr Julian be returning for dinner?"

"No, Maria. He won't." Kate said.

Maria stood hesitantly looking at Kate. "Not till tomorrow then?"

"No. Mr Julian will not be returning," said Kate with finality. "You may go, Maria."

Alice's stomach gave a lurch and Maria's face looked stricken. Maria had always responded coquettishly to his gentle teasing and her smile grew wider whenever he was around.

Maria glanced at Kate and made a hasty exit. Kate poured out the tea in silence.

She handed a cup to Alice. "When did you say you'd be back from Florida?"

"I didn't, but I'll have to be back by the end of October to take possession of the house."

"Hmm, that should work. How would you feel about coming back to Langsmead afterwards?"

"But won't the film crew be here?" said Aice.

"Yes, exactly. I'll be working at the Manville and I need someone to keep an eye on things."

Alice nodded. "Yes, I could do that."

Her new home wouldn't be habitable for many weeks so the arrangement would suit her well enough. Kate still had not mentioned Julian.

"What's going on, Kate?"

"I kicked Julian out."

"Is it over between you?"

She lit a cigarette and took a long draw. "Actually he dumped me."

"Oh, Kate!"

"I thought that once the damned book was finished things would be different but it seems I was wrong."

"I'm so sorry—"

"I tell you, Ali, it hit me like a bloody bombshell!"

It amazed Alice that Kate, so sharp and streetwise, could be so ingenuous in matters of the heart. For a moment she was at a loss for words.

"He was so fucking calm I wanted to hit him. He had the nerve to say he was waiting for the right moment to tell me. It was so bloody humiliating!" She pulled a tissue from her bag and blew her nose noisily. "But then, he was never in love with me. I think I always knew that."

"Are you in love with him, Kate?" asked Alice.

"You can't flog a dead horse."

Kate's pride had taken a bad knock and Alice knew it wasn't sympathy she wanted. A diversion was what was required and when Alice proposed a night on the town, immediately Kate brightened.

"I'll give Suzie a call and tell her to get her butt down here pronto!" she said, leaping up from her chair.

The next morning Alice woke up on the sofa bed in Kate's apartment with a dreadful hangover. She had consumed too many cocktails at Nancy's Bar, the trendy nightclub in the West End where they spent the evening. She padded across the living room into the kitchen. Kate's bedroom door was ajar, but the room was empty and the bed neatly made. She carried a mug of strong coffee back into the living room and sat down on the sofa.

Amongst Kate's acquaintances whom they met at the club was a young man called Fergus. He worked for an investment company in the city and although barely thirty years old he had already made a vast amount of money in hedge funds, both for his company and for himself. Fergus preferred to spend the evening educating Alice in the machinations of the money market than accompanying her on the dance floor. She didn't mind. This was Kate's evening to shine. And shine she did. Alice watched her on the dance floor as she knocked back the cocktails that appeared on the table at regular intervals.

Kate and her partner Marc, a young guy with Latin good looks, were hard to miss. Marc danced with great alacrity and style, tossing Kate up in the air and then passing her between his legs all in one effortless movement. It was such an exhibition that the other dancers moved back to watch them and Kate, wearing a short dress in a shade of plum that perfectly complimented her red hair, was relishing every moment.

Alice hurried breathlessly into Maxie's office. "I'm sorry I'm late."

Maxie looked up from behind her desk and smiled. "Not to worry. No doubt you had a problem with the traffic. Now they've put in that new one-way system, it gets worse by the day."

Alice muttered in agreement knowing full well that Maxine managed to run a home, a husband, two children plus a long train ride yet still be sitting behind her desk looking well-groomed and efficient by nine sharp.

Maxie passed the contract across her desk. "They want completion within a month."

Alice signed the document and handed it back. "Is it going to be a problem?"

"Well, it's going to be tight. You'd better leave me your telephone number in Florida, just in case." she said. "I understand that the vendor is moving abroad and we have to abide by his deadline. You'll need to be back by the completion date."

"Yes, I'm aware of that, Maxie. I'll be back."

By the time Alice left the office her head had cleared, and after collecting her airline ticket, she went to meet Ben to discuss the renovations. They had arranged to rendezvous at a pub in Clapham and as soon as Alice stepped into the crowded saloon bar, she spotted him sitting at a corner table with a striking girl.

He stood up as Alice came over and introduced his companion as Stella. She had huge green eyes, a mass of tawny curls that reached to her shoulders and wore a peasant skirt with a loose cotton top that was at least one size too large for her tiny frame; the effect was very feminine. Stella laughed unaffectedly when Alice told her that she reminded her of a Pre-Raphaelite maiden. She said that her style of dressing was an antidote to the severity of her nurse's uniform and that her clothes were usually purchased from charity shops or car boot sales. Stella was little over five feet tall and looked too young to be a qualified staff nurse.

Alice took an instant liking to Stella and enjoyed her quirky sense of humour. As they became better acquainted, Alice noticed how Stella's Geordie accent became more pronounced when she was upset or nervous.

"Stella has just moved in with me," said Ben.

"He's been keeping me under wraps," said Stella with a laugh. "Doubts that I'll measure up with the family."

"Kate and her mother will love you, Stella!" said Alice.

"Daft girl!" said Ben, landing a smack on her backside as she walked off to the ladies cloakroom.

He turned to Alice. "Look, Ali, this doesn't change anything. The spare room's still yours for as long as you want it."

"Thanks, Ben. It's just for three nights until I leave,"

"I'm very glad you saw sense and went for that house. I know you won't regret it," he said. "And I'll be standing by to start on the renovations as soon as you get completion."

Liking Stella as she did, Alice was disappointed by Kate's condescension when they went to meet her at the hotel the following evening.

"Oh, my God! What a posh joint," said Stella as the uniformed doorman opened the glass outer door and they walked through into the foyer's plush interior. "Am I dressed right for this?"

Alice smiled at her reassuringly. "Bohemian chic? You look great, Stella."

They headed directly to the lounge bar where Kate usually held court. It was a large softly lit room with leather armchairs arranged around the tables and a long modern bar that appeared to carry every type of alcoholic beverage known to man.

Stella rolled her eyes as Alice pointed Kate out, standing amongst the throng of people gathered around the bar. "Ah, so that's sophisticated big sis," said Stella with a nervous giggle. Kate saw them and waved.

Alice took Stella by the arm. "Come on, let's go and sit down."

As soon as they did so a smiling young waiter appeared with glasses of champagne and another followed with a plate of canapés. They were on their second glass when Kate came over, explaining that she was entertaining some guests from New York. It was good to see her looking like her usual bubbly self and Alice marvelled, not for the first time, at her remarkable powers of recovery.

Ben introduced Kate to Stella. Kate's eyes skimmed over her with a quick smile of acknowledgement. Alice took Kate to one side to ask whether it would be all right for her to go to Langsmead to collect the rest of her things.

"Yes, of course you can. I'll give you a set of keys. The house will be empty, you see. Maria and Victor are leaving first thing and I've asked Dave to keep an eye on the place. I'll be down there myself in a couple of days."

Amongst the crowd surrounding Kate, Alice had noticed a tall, good-looking man whom she recognised. "Isn't that Sebastian, the TV guy?" she said.

Kate nodded. "But would you believe this? Felicity is the female lead in his production. It was her idea to shoot at Langsmead all along and she never said a word to me!"

"I suppose you realise that Sebastian can't take his eyes off you," said Alice.

Kate gave a smug smile and the next moment Sebastian was standing beside them with his hand placed on Kate's lower back. He was wearing a fawn jacket in the softest suede Alice had ever seen and she thought he looked rather pleased with himself.

"This is my friend, Alice," said Kate. "She spent the summer with me at Langsmead."

"Ah yes, the efficient little nanny. Hi, there," he said, his voice an affected drawl.

Alice glanced at Kate but someone else had caught her attention. She stared back at a pair of ice-blue eyes.

"Oh, don't look so offended, babe. It's just the way Kate described you. I thought it was amusing."

Alice wasn't in the least offended at the content of his remark. It was his supercilious manner that was offensive. Nor did she care for the way he undressed her with his eyes.

Alice raised her eyebrows. "Do I know you?"

"I'm Sebastian Seth-Smith, the TV director. Kate must have told you about me," he said.

Alice gave a small laugh. "Oh, Kate meets lots of people, you know. I can't remember all of them!"

The champagne kept flowing, but Stella did not look at ease and Ben was strumming his fingers on the table in undisguised boredom. It had been at Alice's suggestion that they came and she had phoned to check it out with Kate but now she realised that it hadn't been one of her better ideas. She glanced from Stella to Ben. "Shall we go?"

Immediately, they were both on their feet, ready to make a retreat. Alice managed to catch Kate's eye and she came over as they were walking out of the bar. She handed Alice the keys. "We're all off to that new Sushi restaurant up the road. Why don't you come along?"

"Dead raw fish! Ugh! You must be joking!" said Stella, screwing up her nose.

Kate rolled her eyes and looked at Ben. In an instinctively protective gesture he put an arm around Stella. "No thanks, Kate. We're out of here."

Alice left with them.

Chapter 16

Langsmead Hall was eerily silent. It was a sunny autumn day but the Grand Hall felt gloomy and oppressive

Maria and Victor had left the place looking spotless. The pine table in the kitchen had been scrubbed to within an inch of its life. Only the quiet hum of the Aga provided a comforting familiarity. Alice made a mug of coffee and as she sat drinking at the kitchen table, she felt a deep sadness. That bubble in time was a thing of memory. Tom, Poppy and Julian were all gone from her life and she must learn to live without them.

She went up to the attic room, gathered up her clothes and a few oddments she had left behind and shoved them into a bag. As she stood on the galleried landing with the bag in her hand she hesitated. The lure of the green bedroom was powerful. She was drawn to it by some magnetic force.

The doll lay on the window seat. Alice picked it up absently, thinking of Poppy's elfin face. She was puzzled to find the doll there. Hadn't Poppy left it on her bed in the attic? Reminded of Julian's speculation, she sat down on the window seat and looked at the doll thoughtfully. As she did so, she became aware that she was not alone.

Eleanor was sitting in front of the dressing table brushing her hair with harsh, impatient strokes. The face that stared at her in the mirror was contorted by anger. How dare Henry force himself upon her so brutally? She shuddered with revulsion at the memory of what had taken place the previous night. Were it not for Declan, she might never have known that the act of love could be such a tender and joyfully sensuous experience, not something that defiled her.

When Mary had brought her tea that morning, she was accompanied by one of the kitchen maids carrying a crystal vase of tall red roses. "Mr Henshaw instructed the gardener to cut the best blooms from the hot house and have them delivered to your room, Ma'am," said Mary.

Outside his work Henry's roses were his chief preoccupation and close to obsession. He inspected them regularly to check they were kept in prime condition for exhibit at the annual horticultural show. Eleanor, on the other hand, liked to see the blooms in a more natural, unrestricted setting, either nestling in the borders or climbing randomly across a wall or pergola, not standing rigidly in rows like soldiers on parade. She stared at the perfect blood-red blooms displayed on her dressing table, grabbed up the crystal vase that contained them and hurled it across the room. It smashed against the wall by the doorway and splintered into fragments. The roses were splayed out across the floor like slain soldiers.

Alice's face was wet with tears. They were tears for both Eleanor and herself. She took out a tissue from her bag, blew her nose and got up to leave. She stared at the doorway and gasped. At first glance she didn't register the tall figure who stood there.

"Julian?"

"Oh, thank God. I've been searching the whole house for you," said Julian.

She rushed across the room and his arms enfolded her. She wished that time would stand still and she could stay for ever in the shelter of those arms.

Later, they sat facing each other at a table in the King's Head public house. Julian reached across the table to take Alice's hand and she glanced around the restaurant self-consciously. There were only a few tables occupied and no one was paying them any attention.

"How did you know I was at the house?"

"I have my spies."

"Tell me."

"Very well," he said, releasing her hand. "I needed to collect a manuscript I left behind and I phoned Dave to check the lay of the land. It was serendipity."

"So Dave told you I was there."

Julian nodded. "He said he was finishing his breakfast when he saw your car drive past his cottage. I got shaved and dressed and hit the motorway as though in a race for my life."

Alice smiled at him over her glass of wine. "I did wonder whether I'd ever see you again."

"You must have known I'd come after you."

"You didn't even say goodbye."

"Hmm. That was tricky."

"Kate was shocked. She didn't expect you to dump her."

"Yes. I made a misjudgement. But I behaved so obnoxiously those last few weeks that I thought she'd be glad to see the back of me."

"You hoped that she would end it herself?"

He nodded. "But I am to blame. I should not have come, never given in to Felicity in the first place. The alternative was to have the children cooped up in my flat for the whole summer and that really wasn't a practical solution. I couldn't think of another."

"But you stayed on after the children left."

"Look, I'm well aware that I over-stayed my welcome by a long chalk and that, too, was unfair to Kate. I was out of order." He gave that crinkly smile Alice liked so much. "But I think you know the reason."

"And I think it's me who's now out of order. I shouldn't be with you like this. Kate wouldn't like it."

"It's no longer her business, remember?"

"Kate is my best friend."

"Could we leave Kate out of this, please? That episode is in the past."

Ted, the pub's landlord, came to their table with two steaming plates of steak and kidney pudding.

Julian refilled their wine glasses and as they ate Alice talked about her forthcoming holiday.

"So you intend to leave in two days' time and plan to be away for one whole month!"

"Yes."

"Cancel it."

"Don't be silly. I can't do that!"

"Yes, cancel it. The book is finished. We can go away together."

They drank more wine and lingered over coffee.

"You know something, Alice. You are infinitely loveable. How I kept my hands off you all summer, I'll never know. I wanted you the first time I laid eyes on you and then when you looked at me with that wistful look of yours..."

"That was at Kate's party."

"Yes. I was just sizing up the bloke you were with when Kate barged in. Had I realised your situation I wouldn't have let anything drag me away. Damned shame!"

He took hold of her hand and kissed it. "Oh, Alice!"

They were gazing into each other's eyes when Ted's wife dropped their bill on the table.

Alice giggled. "We're behaving like a pair of teenagers!"

"Who cares!"

Alice looked around the room and saw that everyone had left.

Dave was walking up the driveway as Julian's car pulled up in front of the house. Alice and Julian stopped to chat to him for a few minutes and then she went on ahead to unlock the entrance door. As she left she heard Julian tell Dave that they would ensure the house was secure before their departure.

"That's fine then," said Dave. "'Cause I'm over to spend the night with my old Dad. He gets ever so lonely without my Ma."

Alice went into the green room to retrieve her bag. The nights were drawing in and inside the room the light was fading. She stood near the bed, looking around the room and feeling its familiar ambience. So recently she had sat on that window seat with her heart in despair. Now her mood was euphoric and she wanted to savour every moment of this unforeseen happiness.

Julian put his head around the door and saw her. "What are you doing?"

"I'm trying to work out what is real and what is not. I think I must be a little drunk."

He smiled and came over to her. "Oh, my adorable girl!"

She reached up her arms and put them around his neck. "I must be the happiest woman on the planet."

"Oh, God, my beautiful Alice," he said hoarsely and pulled her down onto the bed with him.

They kissed long and hungrily and couldn't stop there. The intensity of their passion that night was like nothing Alice had ever experienced. The sun was rising when finally they fell into a heavy sleep.

Alice had a smile on her face as she stretched languidly in the comfortable bed. She reached out her arm and felt the empty space. She knew she hadn't been dreaming because there was an indent on the pillow beside hers. It was then that she noticed the green drapery around the bed and remembered where she was.

The doll still lay on the window seat and after taking a quick shower, Alice took it up to the attic. Afterwards she hurried downstairs.

Julian was standing by the Aga in the kitchen and the table was laid for breakfast He came across the room and kissed her on the lips. "Good morning, sweetheart. How are you?"

She grinned. "Never better."

When he let go of her, she took a step backwards and looked up at him. "But oh my God, what a shock it was to wake up in that bedroom!"

"You may have an even stronger affinity with that room now," he said, chuckling and gestured towards a chair at the table.

Alice shook her head. "Let's go."

"Without even sampling my culinary skills?"

Suddenly she felt nervous. "We shouldn't be here."

"But I went into the village and bought some bacon and eggs. I found some rather nice-looking sausages, too.

You see, I want you to know how well I intend to look after you."

Alice gave in and sat down.

"We'll have our breakfast and afterwards I'm taking you home with me."

"What about my car?"

"We can collect it tomorrow if you like. Let's not worry about such incidentals right now."

Alice laughed. "But you're taking over my life."

"That is the general idea."

"And you've really made a cooked breakfast?"

"It's keeping warm in the oven."

He picked up a cloth, went to the Aga, and opened the top oven door. He lifted out a dish and swore, pulling back his scalded wrist. He dropped the hot dish on the table and stared in horror. "What in the hell has happened?"

Alice looked at the charred morsels of food and grinned. "Oh dear. I'm afraid you put it in the baking oven."

"But it can't have been more than five minutes."

"The warming plate's at the bottom," said Alice.

"Then why didn't I smell the damned thing burning?"

Alice tried hard to keep a straight face. "That's the thing with Agas, you don't smell the cooking."

"Well, there goes our breakfast!"

"We could start again," said Alice, getting up. "Here, let me do it this time."

"No, too late. I've used up all the bacon!" He threw down the cloth and turned to her. "I tell you something, Alice, I'd like to know the person who designed this highly combustible contraption and sue them. It doesn't even carry a warning sign!"

He whipped the dish off the table with such a flourish that half of its contents fell on the floor before reaching the sink.

Alice burst out laughing and bent down to clear up the burnt morsels.

"Get up from the floor, young lady, I'm the one who should be down on his knees!" He grabbed her round the waist and turned her around to face him. "And enough of this giggling. This is no laughing matter!"

But she couldn't stop and nor could he. "This is turning into a farce!" she said.

"More like black comedy!" came a voice behind them.

They turned around to see Kate standing in the doorway. The kitchen was situated at the back of the house and she had made her unobtrusive entry through the front entrance.

Alice took a step back and froze. Julian looked at Kate and smiled. "Good morning, Kate. I'd offer you some breakfast but unfortunately I've just burnt it!"

It seemed he intended to brazen this out. Kate glared at him. "How dare you!" she said, almost spitting out the words.

He kept his tone light. "Hmm. Dare what, Kate?"

Kate was white with rage. "Be here, in this house, in this kitchen!"

"I came to collect my things, Kate" he said evenly. "You threw me out, remember?"

"And Alice, too, well what a coincidence!" said Kate, her voice heavy with sarcasm.

Julian nodded. "Yes, as it happens it was, though I prefer to call it serendipity."

She walked past him and put down her bag on the table, then turned and held out her hand. "I'd like my keys back before you depart."

He went to the sideboard, picked up his key ring and detached two of the keys.

He handed them to her.

Meanwhile, Alice was clearing away all traces of the ill-fated breakfast. She was wiping the floor when she felt Julian's hand on her shoulder. "I think we should leave, Alice."

Alice glanced at Kate and shook her head.

"I didn't ask Alice to leave," said Kate.

He turned to Kate and was about to say something but changed his mind. Kate's expression resembled an angry feline, claws extended.

"I'll have your stuff sent on to you," she said icily.

He picked up the manuscript left on the sideboard. "Alice?" he said, his other hand reaching out to her.

"I can't leave like this, Julian," she said.

"Why don't you get the fuck out of here before I do something I might regret!" Kate snarled through tightly clenched teeth.

"I'll wait in the car, Alice," he said.

Alice nodded.

Kate glanced at Alice and then back at Julian. "If you're not off the premises within five minutes, I'll be calling the police."

He stood by the door. "This is ridiculous, Kate."

Alice bit hard on her lower lip to stop the tears welling up. "I'll see you later, Julian."

As soon as he walked out of the door Kate went to the sideboard and calmly measured ground coffee into the cafetière. She held it aloft and glanced at Alice.

She nodded and stood watching Kate, her hands clenched over the back of a chair. "I don't know what to say, Kate, except that I'm very sorry you had to witness this."

"Is that all you have to say?" she said and sat down at the table.

She gave Alice a hostile stare. "Well, you snake in the grass. What a fine friend you've turned out to be. Perfidious is the adjective that comes to mind." She paused for a moment. "So you're not sorry about having this sordid little affair behind my back?"

"We haven't been having an affair, Kate."

"So what would you call it?"

"As Julian said, it was a coincidence we were both here yesterday."

"Oh, just a one night stand, was it? That doesn't sound like you. Still, he's pretty good in the shagging department, isn't he? I expect we can agree upon that."

Alice winced and retreated to the doorway. "I'll get my things and go."

"I suppose you think I should be glad it was my best friend and not a tart like Suzie? Would that be more or less humiliating, I wonder."

Kate knew how to aim her darts. Alice leant back against the door frame for support. "For God's sake, Kate, stop it!" she yelled at her.

Suddenly Kate burst into tears. "I'm sorry. I'm sorry. It's the shock! It's making me say things I don't mean."

She held out her arms. "Please don't go. We've been through so much together and our friendship means everything to me," she said sobbing again. "You're like a sister to me. I don't want to lose you like this."

There were some paper napkins on the table and Alice handed her one. She wiped her eyes and blew her nose. Alice gave her a quick hug and they both sat down.

"You were fooling around like a couple of teenagers, that's what really rattled me. We never had that kind of fun," Kate said with a sniff.

Alice stared down into her coffee mug.

"Different sense of humour I suppose but then I've never found absurdity in the least bit amusing," she said. "Sorry, I'm starting again!"

Alice was wondering whether Julian had left and her head started to throb.

As though reading her thoughts, Kate got up and left the room. She returned a few minutes later. "He's gone," she said, a hint of triumph in her voice.

Alice's hands were trembling and she had to pick up her mug with both hands.

Kate glanced across at her. "I realise I should never have got involved with the egocentric shit in the first place, but as for making out with my best friend, I never thought he'd stoop that low."

"I told you before, Kate. It wasn't planned."

"Well I guess we are both in shock, but I want you to know that it's not you I blame. What with the kids and everything, you were thrown so much together it's no wonder you became infatuated and fell for his charms. I wasn't around enough, was I?"

Alice nodded.

"Well, I know what men are like, the bastards," she said.

Alice wanted to say that she was equally to blame but the words wouldn't come. Kate had taken control of the situation and in doing so had regained her composure.

It was a relief when the telephone rang and Kate left the room to answer it. Alice sat there in total misery. The magic of the last twenty-four hours had been severed so suddenly and shockingly that her brain had gone numb.

She looked up as Kate came back into the room. Kate's expression was much brighter.

"That was Sebastian. Someone at the Manville must have told him I was here. I told him to stop stalking me!" Kate said. She sat down again and picked up her coffee mug. "Pity he's so young."

Alice struggled to focus on what she was saying. "Oh, Sebastian. How old is he?"

"I found out the other day that he's only twenty-nine."

"He looks older."

"Yes, he does, doesn't he?" said Kate. "Well, as I was saying, we're not going to have one night of shagging jeopardise all our years of friendship, are we"?"

"No, Kate."

"So I'd like to draw a line under this morning and put it behind us."

Alice nodded and managed a small smile.

"For us it's friendship first. Right?"

If this was what Kate wanted Alice was in no mood to argue.

Alice didn't leave until the afternoon and the two-hour journey to London passed in a blur. It took all her concentration to focus on driving. Kate had explained that the purpose of her visit was to meet some wedding caterers and at her request, Alice stayed until they arrived. It seemed to her the least she could do. Kate was her closest friend and in Kate's eyes she had betrayed their friendship in the worst possible way. What madness had possessed her to imagine for one moment that she and Julian could ride roughshod over Kate's feelings. Any future together was out of the question.

By the time Alice came off the motorway she was exhausted and it took the last of her energy to negotiate the roads to Clapham. It was almost six o'clock by the time she reached Ben's flat. She planned to go straight to bed and turned the key in the lock with a sigh of relief.

She was walking across the hallway towards the spare room when she heard Stella's voice. "Is that you, Ben?"

Alice pushed open the door into the living room. "No, it's me, Alice."

"Hi, Alice," said Stella.

She was standing in front of a mirror taking out the clips that held up her hair. It tumbled down over her shoulders and she gave it a shake. "I've just come off a shift," she said, turning around.

Alice stepped into the room and Stella stared at her. "You look crap!"

"Thanks," said Alice, going over to give her a peck on the cheek.

"What's the matter?" she said, her voice full of concern.

Alice shrugged. "Bad day."

"Well, mine wasn't so hot either," she said. "You come and sit down. I'm going to make us a nice pot of tea."

The living room extended into a very well-appointed modern kitchen, creating a large, airy space. While she put on the kettle and warmed the teapot, Stella described an altercation with one of the young doctors.

"Silly prick can't take no for an answer. He's fresh out of medical school and thinks he's God's gift to women!" she said, handing Alice a mug of hot, strong tea.

Alice thought of Sebastian. "I met someone like that when we went to see Kate. I just hope she doesn't get too involved with him," she said, sipping the tea appreciatively.

She watched Stella stirring eggs in a pan. "You look like you need something to eat," she said, buttering slices of toast.

"That's good of you, Stella. As a matter of fact I've eaten nothing all day."

She put a tray on Alice's lap and she ate up the scrambled eggs on toast without really tasting them.

Afterwards Stella sat down beside her on the sofa. "So, what's happened to you?"

"I was down at the hotel with Kate's ex-boyfriend," said Alice.

"Yes. We wondered why you didn't turn up last night," she said. "I suppose this ex turned out to be a shit."

"Oh no, he didn't. But unfortunately Kate turned up unexpectedly."

"Oh, dear me!" she said with a chuckle. "A ménage à trois!"

"God no!"

"So she wasn't overjoyed to find you with her ex-lover?"

"Kate was incandescent with rage and threw him out," said Alice.

"She didn't throw you out, too?"

"No, but I got a real dressing down,"

"Oh, poor you! I wouldn't like to cross swords with that lady!"

Stella quickly wheedled the whole story out of her and it was such an immense relief to pour it all out that she ended up sobbing on Stella's shoulder.

"Oh, you poor lass!" she said, running off to get a box of tissues and a shot of whisky for them both.

"There was a call for you earlier. A male of mature years with a nice deep voice."

"Oh, I don't remember telling him I was staying here," said Alice, agitated.

"If it was him, he must be keen enough to track you down," Stella said.

"What did you say?"

"Just that you weren't here. He left a number. I've written it down somewhere," she said. "I'll go and find it if you like."

Alice shook her head.

"Fine," she said. "But take my advice and don't you let anyone pressure you into doing what you don't want to do."

"Why do you say that?"

"'Cause it looks to me like you could be a pushover," she said with a laugh.

Alice looked at her and smiled. "I'll try and remember that."

Stella agreed that a good night's sleep was what Alice needed. She bustled about the spare room making sure Alice had all she needed and then gave her a hot milky drink and a sleeping pill.

Stella wasn't working the following day and had been up for several hours before Alice made an appearance at midday.

"How are you, love?" Stella asked, looking up from her ironing.

Alice grimaced. "Groggy!"

Stella carefully folded the uniform dress laid out on the ironing board. "Well, you sit down and I'll make us a cuppa. After that I'm planning on a trip to Covent Garden. How's that with you?"

Alice nodded and sat down on the sofa. "Sounds good to me." At that moment she felt so numb that she would have gone anywhere that Stella suggested.

The sun was shining as they sat at the pavement café table drinking their coffee and watching the world go by. People were strolling around, chatting, laughing and absorbing the square's lively atmosphere. Alice was surprised to find herself laughing at the silly antics of a pair of street entertainers.

"Now, that's better," said Stella, patting Alice's hand.

Alice turned and smiled at her ruefully. "Yes. Life goes on."

"And you never know what's waiting around the corner," said Stella.

After checking in her luggage at Heathrow Airport Alice looked for a telephone booth. First she made a brief call to Kate, then pulled out a crumpled piece of paper from her pocket. She stared at Julian's number. This call could not be evaded any longer.

"Oh, Alice, darling girl. It's so good to hear your voice," he said down the line. "I waited for you for over an hour. Are you all right? I've been worried about you,"

"Yes, I'm okay. What about you?"

"Just holding on until I can see you. Let me come and pick you up. Where are you?"

Alice took a deep breath and told him that she was at the airport.

"It's Kate, isn't it?" he said. "I suppose she put you through the wringer."

"Probably no more than I deserved."

"I can't take that seriously."

"We've hurt her badly. Kate's more vulnerable than you think."

"If the shoe were on the other foot, I can assure you she would have no such scruples. Kate is ruthless. But look, let's not argue about it. What I want you to do right now is to stop and think about what you're doing."

"I've done that. Please don't make this any harder."

"Are you really prepared to throw away something so God-damned special because of your friendship with Kate?"

"I've got to go. If I don't go through customs now I'll miss my flight. It leaves in thirty five minutes."

"Then miss it. I'll come and collect you."

"No. I'm really sorry, Julian.

"Oh, Alice. Don't do this."

She heard him say something else but he spoke too softly and the line began to crackle. Alice replaced the receiver.

Julian sat in his study with the receiver to his ear. "Don't go, Alice. I love you."

The line went dead. He stared in bewilderment at the receiver he still held, then glanced at his watch. He let out an anguished groan.

Chapter 17

Erin was waiting behind the barrier at Sanford Airport's arrivals terminal and greeted Alice effusively. She wheeled her trolley to the car park and put her luggage into the trunk of a dark blue Mercedes convertible.

"Jump in," she said, opening the passenger seat door.

"Make yourself comfortable 'cause you've got a three-hour journey ahead."

"That's a lot of driving for you, Erin. I should have transferred to the local airport," said Alice, getting into the car.

"No way. You don't need all that hassle. Besides, this gave me an excuse to try out Dad's new car," said Erin, revving up the engine.

The roof was down and the wind whipped through their hair as they sped along the highway. After an hour or so, Erin pulled in to a Comfort inn.

Alice sipped at the coffee the waitress had poured and took a drink of water.

"Insipid, huh?" said Erin.

Alice nodded. "You get the best breakfast in the world in this country but forget about the coffee!"

"Yeah, it's always the same in these places. You'll get the real thing in Naples."

Alice sat back and looked at Erin's glowing face. "You're looking really well, Erin."

"Yeah, thanks. I'm feeling pretty good."

"So how's Steve?"

"Steve – oh, he's history! We broke up when I came back from Europe. He was a jerk, Alice. The bastard was screwing my best friend Beth the whole time I was away. Can you believe that?"

This piece of news struck too close to home and Alice bit her lip. "Well, I bet your Mum is pleased."

Erin laughed. "Yeah, sure she was. We're on speaking terms again. Now that I'm dating Alex I can do no wrong."

"What's so special about Alex?"

"He's a lawyer."

"Oh, a lawyer, eh? So where did you meet him?"

"It was on the plane going home, would you believe it? He'd been on a business trip to London. Turns out that Dad knew his boss and then Alex and I started chatting. We clicked straight away."

"Is it serious?"

"He's just asked me to marry him."

"Good Gracious! That was quick!!"

"You know what it's like when you meet the right person. We both knew straight away."

"Well, congratulations, Erin," said Alice. "So your mum must be happy. What about your dad?"

"Mom doesn't know about the engagement yet but she'll probably be over the moon," she said. "And you know Dad, he'll be happy so long as I am."

"Who does Alex work for?"

"One of the big Texan oil corporations, you can't get more respectable than that!" said Erin, laughing. "Pa is a bit concerned about the speed of it all so I promised him

166

we'd wait a year before getting hitched. The thing is, Alex's company have offered him a job in their London branch and I want to go with him."

"What! You're coming to London?"

"Yes, that's the plan. It's their European head office. He'll be dealing with contracts in the Middle East and Russia. It's a great career move."

"They must think very highly of him."

"Yeah, he's doing okay. Alex is real cool. I know you're going to like him."

Alice nodded and took a mouthful of pizza.

"Tell me about you, Alice. What have you been up to?"

"Well, I'm buying a house in south London."

"That's neat. Hey, I might well turn out to be your first house guest. I'm planning to come over to look for an apartment, you see."

Art's holiday home was a Spanish-style villa built in white stucco work and surrounded by a beautifully landscaped garden stocked with exotic tropical plants.

When the car pulled up in the driveway, Art came out to greet them. He was dressed in a sweatshirt and jogging pants and looked very fit. "Hi honey," he said to Erin. "You've made better time than I thought, I was about to go for a jog."

He gave Alice a hug and lifted her suitcase out of the car. "Is this a body you've got in here?" he grinned, taking hold of the bag she was carrying.

"I'm sorry. It's my easel and sketch books. Just as well I didn't bring the oils. I thought I might do some painting while I'm here."

"If you enjoy seascapes, you've come to the right place," he said, leading her into a large airy hallway.

Erin went off to phone Alex and Alice followed Art along the passage into a living room. It was decorated and furnished in pretty shades of pastel. A pair of sliding doors led into the bedroom and along the length of both rooms was a balcony facing out to the ocean.

Alice stared at the spectacular views. "Is this all for me?" she said, laughing.

"I hope you like it," he said, depositing her luggage in the bedroom. "When you've rested up a bit, you might like to stretch your legs and take a look around."

Alice was too keyed up to rest and ten minutes later she ventured out of the suite. Art was sitting on the terrace reading a newspaper. "So you're ready for the grand tour, are you?" he asked, getting up. "First let's get you a nice cold drink."

A good-looking, dark-haired boy appeared as though awaiting his cue. Art turned and put an arm around the boy's shoulder. "This is Jaime, originally from Mexico, though he's spent most of his life here in Florida."

The boy stepped forward to shake her hand. "Alice is our guest from England, Jaime. I'd like you to help me take care of her," said Art.

Jaime smiled shyly and promptly went off to fetch her drink.

The swimming pool was situated behind a high brick wall and adjacent to it was a single-storey building that housed a gymnasium.

Alice's gaze lingered on the pool's aquamarine water. "If you fancy a swim, you'll find all you need in there," said Art, gesturing to the building behind them.

"But first, let me take you to see the ocean."

The back yard led down to a wide area of decking stretching down to the waterfront.

"The Gulf of Mexico," he announced, spreading his arms wide.

Alice was taken aback by the sight of the wide blue ocean.

"Not so bad, eh?" he grinned.

"It's a paradise, Art."

"Yeah, I spend as much time around here as I can."

Alice gazed out at the small boats bobbing gently on the water. "My favourite childhood holidays were spent by the sea, though I'm afraid the old English Channel can't quite compete with this!"

"I tried swimming in your English Channel once. I thought the water was going to freeze off my... Let's just say it was cold!" he chuckled.

She gestured to the handsome 40-foot yacht moored off the jetty. "Is that yours?"

"That is Christabel. Now, she is my real pride and joy."

As she would later discover, the yacht's interior was luxuriously appointed and equipped with all the most modern technology.

Art and Erin could not have been more welcoming, but for the first three days Alice kept mostly to her room. She would come out for a swim in the pool, eat a little lunch and afterwards, pleading jet lag, retreat to the suite. She tried to obliterate the recent events from her mind but it was impossible.

Kate had described Alice's feelings for Julian as 'infatuation' but she was wrong. Alice knew that infatuation was something different entirely. She could never regret that night with Julian in spite of the consequences. Kate's anger was shocking but Alice believed it was justified. She had betrayed her best friend in the worst possible way and put their friendship in jeopardy. But if she could turn back the clock, would she have made that phone call from the airport? She believed he was telling her that he loved her before she put down the phone. How she longed to tell him that she loved him, too. Alice sobbed into those soft pillows until sleep overcame her.

On the fourth morning Erin knocked on the door to the suite at 7.30. Alice scrambled out of bed and opened the door. "Come on, Alice," she ordered. "Get your swimming gear together. We're going out on the boat."

On this first trip out to sea, Erin told Alice that the vessel was the third Christabel to be moored off their jetty, each named after Art's mother.

"Pop really worshipped his Mom," Erin told her. "He says that everything he's achieved is down to her. Apparently she sacrificed a lot to get her two boys through college, and the one thing that saddens him is that she didn't live long enough to enjoy the rewards."

Alice was to become very familiar with the boat since most of the holiday revolved around excursions to the Gulf's picturesque islands and their sandy white beaches. Most days they set off in the morning and anchored near a reef to swim or go snorkelling and later returned for a long, lazy lunch on board. Jaime, who usually accompanied them on these trips, was always on hand to help serve the seafood or what other delicacies were produced from the well-stocked fridge.

Jaime had bright brown eyes and a cheerful disposition. Alice learned that during his vacations Jaime was officially an employee though treated by Art and Erin as a member of the family. Like them, Jaime was very competent in the water. Erin also told her that his Mexican mother Consuela had been employed at the villa for the last nineteen years and was now the resident housekeeper. She went on to describe how Connie, as she called her, had arrived with Jaime, her six-month-old baby, strapped on her back and that subsequently Art had taken responsibility for getting Jaime through school and currently through college.

One morning when Alice was helping Jaime to carry the scuba diving equipment on board he suggested that she should try diving.

She shook her head. "No, Jaime, I think I'll pass on this one."

Art, who was stowing away the helmets in the hold, glanced round at her. "Have you done any diving, Alice?"

"No, Art. I've never tried."

"You'll soon get the hang of it."

Art would brook no argument and before they left the bay, he took her into the shallow water and coerced her into experimenting with the diving gear. He ran her through the procedure with great diligence, willing her on until she got the hang of it. "You can trust me, Alice," he grinned. "When I was a student, I spent the whole summer season in Hawaii working as a diving instructor."

Two hours later they were moored off Marco Island. Alice watched Erin jump off the boat and disappear into the water. "Come on, Alice, it's your turn now," Jaime said with a grin.

Alice sat hesitantly on the edge of the boat. "Nothing to worry about, Jaime will be right there beside you," said Art, coaxingly.

After her second dive, Art helped her up into the boat. "What did I tell you?" he said with a self-satisfied grin. "You're a natural, a real water baby."

Alice took off the headgear and laughed. "I think I could get addicted to this! It's like being transported into another world. I just had no idea of the beauty and tranquillity of the sea bed. "

"Not so tranquil if you're one of those little fish about to be swallowed up by a huge great predator," he chuckled.

The days slipped by and after three and a half weeks of this idyllic life Alice was fit and tanned and feeling renewed. The memory of Julian and those last traumatic days in England were no longer so tortuous. The stabbing pain had morphed into the occasional dull throb.

One evening as she lay on the deck soaking up the late sunshine she confided in Erin for the first time.

"Here we go, it's cocktail time," said Erin, coming up beside her and holding out a highball glass.

Erin was wearing a bright yellow t-shirt over her bikini, and with her long raven hair, high cheek bones and lithe tanned body, she reminded Alice of an exotic bird of paradise.

She handed Alice the glass. "Dad's with the Proctors. They've just come aboard. Joan and Terry have the next house along the bay and they're here for the weekend. Dad's telling them his plans for the engagement party."

Erin settled down on a towel beside her." You're getting a gorgeous golden tan, Alice," said Erin. "I guess the folks back home are going to be envious!"

Alice smiled smugly. "Hmm, I heard on the news that it's cold and very wet in London."

"I really dig London. It's such a buzzing city," she said. "Is that where you're heading when you get back?"

"No. I'm going to Langsmead. I promised Kate I'd help out there for a bit."

"You know, I often think about that house. It made a real impact on me."

"Yes, I remember."

"Did I ever tell you about my nocturnal visitor?"

Alice glanced at her with interest. "No. You didn't."

"It came two nights in a row. Pop said I was hallucinating, but I wasn't on anything. I didn't score at all on that whole trip and I know it was no mortal who entered that room."

"Yes, I've been accused of hallucinating, too," said Alice with a grin. "Erin, you slept in the green bedroom in the east wing, didn't you?"

"Yeah, I guess so. The furnishings were all green and very pretty, too."

"That room is significant. It was once her room, Eleanor's room."

"Eleanor?"

"Do you remember me telling you about those children who drowned in the lake?"

"Yeah. Yeah, I remember."

"Eleanor was their mother."

"So it's she who haunts that room?"

Alice talked of her unusual connection to Eleanor and everything that she had learned about her.

"My God, Alice, that is so extraordinary!" Erin said when she finished. "Weird how you've gotten so involved in this dead woman's life."

"Yes, you're right and I can't explain it. Julian thought I was obsessed."

"Oh, yeah, Julian, I remember him. He was a cute guy."

As soon as she'd mentioned his name, she regretted it.

Erin glanced over at Alice. "And how is he?"

"Um, he's okay. He's just finished his novel."

"Until you told me otherwise, Pop and I thought that you and Julian had something going."

"We almost did."

"And you let him go?"

"I had to. I didn't have much choice."

"Is that what the reticence is all about?"

"What do you mean?"

"It's about him, isn't it? That first week you were here I was worried about you. There were times when you looked like you were carrying a huge burden, a burden you weren't prepared to share."

"You're very perceptive, Erin."

"Oh, Dad was worried about you, too. I was hoping you'd confide in me but didn't like to intrude."

"And you deserve an explanation," said Alice. She repeated the sorry saga about Julian, Kate and herself just as she had told it to Stella, though this time it was without the tears.

When Alice told her about the phone call, Erin raised her eyebrows. "So he believed your loyalty to Kate was misplaced, did he?" she said. "And what do you think?"

"I really don't know any more," said Alice. "My mother once accused me of the same thing though in a very different context. She put it down to my stubbornness."

"Maybe you just like to be true to your own convictions?"

"I can be very stubborn."

"You aren't alone there," said Erin with a grin. "Hey, did I tell you I've been looking into my Mom's genealogy and that her folks emigrated from England back at the beginning of this century."

"Oh, where were they from?" asked Alice.

"Don't know that yet but I've traced her back to a couple called Mr and Mrs Herbert Nicholson. They were her grandparents. My Mom has never talked about them, never once mentioned any of her relatives except of course for her mother, Lydia. She often talks about her."

"You may discover you've got some living relatives across the big pond."

"Wouldn't that be something!"

Art approached across the deck. With him were Joan and Terence Proctor.

"How are you girls doing?" he asked.

"Just great, Dad," said Erin. "We've been discussing the ghost at Langsmead."

Art winked at Alice conspiratorially. "I'm afraid my daughter believes that all old houses are haunted."

"So where's this new man of yours, Erin?" asked Joan. "Your father's just been telling us about the engagement. We're all very excited for you."

"Thanks, Joan," Erin smiled at her. "You'll get to meet him on the weekend."

Chapter 18

"Hi, Alice," said Art, coming up behind her on the decking. "Jaime told me you were out here. I thought you might fancy some refreshment."

Alice had come out early to catch the early morning light and was sitting behind her easel painting a watercolour of the yachts bobbing on the water.

She turned around and stared at Art in surprise. He was dressed in a suit and tie in place of his everyday casual attire. "You look very formal, Art," she said.

"Yes, I'm flying off to Chicago in an hour," he said, handing her a mug of coffee. "I try to avoid business meetings during the vacation, but unfortunately I've got to see my lawyers about a new contract." He gestured towards Alice's easel. "May I take a look?"

Alice nodded and looked self-consciously at the painting. "You'll have to make allowances. It's the first time I've attempted boats. They look a bit primitive."

"You shouldn't be so modest. I like its naiveté."

"Thank you."

"Hmm, you've given the Gulf a flavour of the sunny Mediterranean. It makes me think of Matisse."

"He's one of my favourite painters."

"I'm fortunate enough to be the owner of two Matisse paintings. I keep them in my Manhattan apartment. You'll have to come and take a look at them one day. They're really rather special."

Alice was as much impressed by this disclosure as by his attitude. Others might boast about the possession of such treasures but that wasn't Art's way.

"When Erin emerges, will you tell her that I'll be back late tonight or first thing tomorrow. I believe Alex is coming along later so you won't be short of company." He turned to leave, then looked back and smiled at her. "You have a good day, Alice. And stick with the painting. You're doing very well."

Alex was almost thirty. He was tall with Nordic good looks and a self-assured manner that lacked affectation. Like most lawyers, he enjoyed a good debate and always had a point of view but at the same time he could be funny and self-deprecating.

That weekend the Proctors held a barbecue in their backyard. Joan was a conscientious hostess and made Alice feel welcome. It was a very warm day and as they stood chatting under the shade of a tall palm tree, they watched Erin and Alex together on the croquet lawn. He stood behind her demonstrating how the mallet should be held, but then Erin started clowning around and they fell over on the grass with Erin in fits of giggles.

"Erin's behaving just like she did as a kid," said Joan, smiling indulgently. "She used to fool around like that with my boys."

"They look really happy," said Alice.

"Yeah, they sure do," Joan nodded. "Of course I'd been hoping that Erin and my boy Jason might become an item." She gave a small sigh. "Still, it wasn't to be."

Joan was an attractive, well-preserved woman of about fifty and slim as a greyhound. Her stylish shorts showed off her slender tanned legs and everything about her was taut and toned. She confided to Alice that in her youth she'd been unfashionably plump. "My current shape is entirely due to a strict regime of a non-fat diet and daily workouts in the gym!" she laughed. "We have our own gym in the New York apartment block. That's where we live most of the year."

The Procters' house was about half a mile further along the bay from Art's property, and like his, it was designed in the style of a Spanish villa. "We bought the house about twenty years back, a year after Art bought his," she told me. "One weekend he and Marion invited us to stay and we fell in love with the area."

"So you and Art go back a long way? Said Alice.

"Oh, yeah, Terry and Art have been friends since college days and I was dating Terry when I first met Art. It was before he got married to Marion and if I hadn't already been involved with Terry, I'd have set my cap at him," she said with a grin. "I've always had a soft spot for Art."

"I'm quite overwhelmed by his hospitality," said Alice.

"Yes. Art is a generous man. He's a very loyal friend, too. And, Erin, of course, is a chip off the old block."

"Oh, yes, I can see that."

"Not like her mother at all. Marion was a snob and I never really took to her. I think Art was well rid of her. Surprising though that he hasn't got married again."

Joan was an inquisitive as well as a talkative woman and Alice soon found herself divulging her experiences as Humphrey's PA.

"Oh, Gary, come hear this," said Joan, calling out to a boy amongst the group of young people nearby.

Joan's younger son Gary, as well as most of his friends, turned out to be ardent Ron Humphrey fans and had attended the concerts on his US tours. Unwittingly, Alice found herself the focus of attention as they gathered around firing questions about his most recent recordings.

Alice was rescued by Erin. "Time to get some lunch, honey," she said, taking her arm and walking them off to the barbecue.

Alice stared at the wide selection of fish. "Try this," said Erin, scooping up an unfamiliar fish and putting in on her plate. "It's local and very good."

"Looks like you've made a hit with the guys!" Erin laughed,

"More like Ron Humphrey is the main attraction. The fact is they know more about Humphrey's music than I ever did!" said Alice. "I was far too busy taking care of his domestic arrangements to spend much time in a recording studio."

"That guy Jay asked me whether you'd like to go kayaking with them," said Erin with a smirk.

They were a nice bunch of kids, but they did make Alice feel every one of her thirty-four years. She glanced back over her shoulder and noticed Jay looking in her direction. He towered over the others by at least half a foot and was hard to miss. He nodded and grinned at her.

"It's that accent of yours. The guys just dig it," said Erin. "As a matter of fact, I thought we might take a couple of kayaks down the waterways ourselves tomorrow. The nature there is pretty spectacular. I think you'd enjoy it."

Lunch tables were set up under the shade of a vine-covered pergola at the back of the villa.

Art stood up. "Ah, I see Erin found you," he said to Alice, pulling out the chair next to him.

"Alice was about to be swallowed up by Jay," said Erin with a laugh.

A ripple of laughter went round the table and Erin explained to her that Jay was the local basketball hero.

"He's also the local heart-throb," said Joan with a titter.

"Jay's been our big white hope for some while now, Alice. His parents are good friends," said Terry, getting up and pouring out the wine. He gestured to the serving boy to bring some more beer and then glanced around at his guests. "I heard from Dom the other day that Miami Heat may be signing him up."

"Oh, Terry, won't that be great!" said Joan. "Dom will be so proud."

Alex leaned across towards Alice. "I don't believe basketball is a popular sport in the UK, is it?"

"No, it's all football and rugby, and cricket of course," said Alice.

Terry sat down again and glanced across at her. "We were just discussing your prime minister and the miracles she's performed with the economy."

"I don't think our high employment figures are much to be proud of," said Alice.

"I thought you Brits were enjoying the new prosperity," said Alex.

"I doubt the miners would agree with that, Alex," said Art. "The closure of the coal mines has caused untold poverty and hardship."

Alice turned to him and nodded. "Power has gone to Thatcher's head. People are saying it's time she went."

"So are you a political animal, Alice?" said Alex.

"'Afraid not, Alex," said Alice. "This is personal, you see. My grandmother grew up in a Yorkshire mining community and it would have broken her heart to witness what's happened."

Alex raised his eyebrows. "And after all Maggie's done, you'd rather have the Socialists back in?"

"I usually vote Green!" said Alice with a smile.

"Isn't that what you'd call opting out?" said Alex.

"Not if you care about the environment, Alex," said Art.

Erin turned to Alex who sat on the chair beside her. "That's something Dad's serious about. His factories are pioneering biodegradable materials."

"One day it could become mandatory," Art said.

"The environment is definitely not a priority on this government's agenda, nor is it likely to be," said Terry.

"It's time we woke up Terry, or it'll be too late," Art said. "I'm ashamed to think of the legacy that we're passing on to the next generation."

"Oh, you're so right, Art!" said Joan. "Do you know, I read in the paper this morning that in the Florida region alone, pollution has almost doubled since the '50s!"

"My God, that's happened in just thirty years!" said Erin.

"We live in a selfish society, sweetheart," said Art.

"You should go into politics, Dad," she said.

Art shook his head and laughed.

"But I'm serious, Dad. We need people who'll take action."

Terry nodded. "She's right, you know, Art."

"Yes, Dad, you'd know how to kick ass!"

Art chuckled. "Steady there, honey. Next you'll have me running for Governor!"

The days of the glorious Florida sunshine passed all too quickly and with the last day of her holiday approaching, Alice dug out her airline ticket and realised she was leaving on the day of the engagement party.

A few moments later when Erin appeared to see whether she was ready to go kayaking, Alice was staring at the ticket in dismay.

She held out the ticket. "I have made a stupid mistake – I'm leaving on the 30th not the 31st."

"But you can't miss the party. I insist you stay!"

Erin went into the living room to find Art. "Dad, Alice is threatening to boycott the party!"

Art looked up from his newspaper. "Surely not."

He got up and came out of the room to where Alice was standing in the hallway.

"It would mean a good deal to us to have you stay, Alice," he said.

Erin took hold of the ticket and handed it to him. "You could get this changed, couldn't you, Dad?"

Alice hadn't considered that option. "No, no, Erin," she said.

Art winked at Alice. "Just one day, right?" he said and walked off with the ticket.

Alice looked at Erin indignantly. "You have a darn nerve!"

Later, Alice was grateful for Erin's high handedness because the party was spectacular, an event that she should have been loath to miss.

The two party planners had arrived the previous day to oversee the erection of a huge marquee and the following morning Alice watched a truckload of food and other incidentals arrive at the house. Alex's parents and a host of friends from around the country were flown in for the occasion. Only Erin's mother had turned down the invitation on the grounds that she would be holding a separate celebration.

At the top table in the marquee Art was seated between Madeleine, Alex's mother, and Erin. Bradley, Alex's father sat on the other side of Erin with Alice beside him. He was a big, friendly Texan and conversation flowed easily between them. Art looked in his element. He had appeared earlier looking very dapper in a cream tuxedo and being a naturally gregarious man, he was an excellent host. His gaiety was infectious.

After the meal, he got up to make a toast to his daughter and her fiancé. It was a short, funny speech and the audience applauded appreciatively, but afterwards and much to Alice's consternation, he put the focus on her.

"We're lucky enough to have our friend Alice with us today. It's been a pleasure to have her as a house guest and I'd like you all to raise your glasses to our lovely English rose!"

Alice was startled to be suddenly singled out and with a hundred pairs of strangers' eyes upon her, she nodded and raised her glass to him. Afterwards the dancing began with Erin and Alex first on the floor and followed by Art with Madeleine. Alice was partnered by several of the guests in turn and when the band blasted out a rock 'n roll number, Erin and Alex performed such an energetic routine that Alice feared her white fitted dress might split at any moment.

As they passed on the dance floor Art whispered in Alice's ear. "You're to save the next one for me!"

The band started to play 'Fly me to the moon' and the young male singer gave a rendition of which Sinatra himself would not have been ashamed. Art whisked Alice onto the floor and as he took her in his arms, his cheek brushed against hers. He pulled her close and for a few moments he closed his eyes.

Erin passed by and smirked. "Oh, Dad, what an old sentimentalist you are!" She winked at Alice. "It's one of his all-time favourites."

By two o'clock the guests were making an exit. Erin and Alex had disappeared and Alice slipped back to her room to change out of her favourite blue frock. Dressed in shorts and a t-shirt, she walked off down to the waterfront. The evening had been a great climax to her visit and she wanted one last look at the ocean.

The lights on the decking shimmered across the water and the sky was speckled with a myriad bright stars. She stood listening to the rhythmic patter of the waves lapping on the shore and, throwing off her shoes, she stepped across the sand and into the shallow water. It was time to face up to the reality of tomorrow. What would that bring? Would she still be in thrall to Eleanor when she returned to Langsmead Hall? For a brief moment she allowed herself to think of those twenty-four hours with Julian and as a wave of nostalgia washed over her, she heard a soft footfall on the sand.

"Sorry if I startled you, but I saw this silhouette in the water and thought it was a mermaid!" Art said with a grin.

"Just a mere mortal, I'm afraid,"

He waded towards her through the water. She turned to him and smiled. "It's so very beautiful here."

"You don't have to leave, you know."

"Don't tempt me, Art. I think I've been thoroughly spoilt this last month. I could too easily get accustomed to it," said Alice.

Art now stood facing her. "Then why don't you?"

She laughed. "What, stay in Florida?"

"Yes. You could stay here and marry me."

She looked at his white trouser bottoms flapping in the water and fought the urge to burst into a fit of giggles. "Art, you've still got your shoes on! You're soaked!"

He followed her out of the water and picked up her discarded shoes. "I'm a clumsy bastard to spring something like that on you," he said, handing her the shoes. "What would a lovely girl like you want with a balding fifty-five year old American? I'm sorry if I've embarrassed you. I don't know what got into me."

"You haven't embarrassed me, Art." said Alice and took his arm.

They walked barefoot back to the villa.

At nine o'clock the following morning Art was waiting for her beside the dark blue Mercedes. Jaime carried her luggage and Alice followed him out of the villa. Suddenly Erin dashed up behind her. Her hair was tousled and she wore an inside out t-shirt and shorts. They hugged each other tightly. "See you in London!" she said.

Art greeted Alice in his usual cheery manner, but as they drove off and onto the highway, he was unusually subdued.

After a few miles Alice broke the silence. "That was a really fantastic party, Art. I'm so glad I didn't miss it."

Art shifted in his seat. "I hope my behaviour didn't spoil your evening. I'm afraid the alcohol brought out the whimsy in me."

He turned his head to glance at her and she could see the anxiety in his kind blue eyes. For a moment he looked so vulnerable that had she been in a position to do so, she would have given him a reassuring hug.

She rested her hand on his knee for a moment. "Absolutely not, Art, I had a wonderful time."

He gave a rueful smile. "I come from Irish immigrant stock, third generation, and though my grandfather diluted the blood by marrying a Cherokee Indian, the Irish peasant can still rear its uncouth head."

"That's nonsense, Art. You've never behaved other than the perfect gentleman!" said Alice with a laugh.

After her luggage was checked in at the terminal, Alice turned to Art to say goodbye. He stood stiffly in front her and stretched out his hand.

"Do we have to be so formal?" she said and held out her arms to give him a hug. His arms wrapped around her and held her for a moment. "I...we're going to miss that funny accent of yours."

"And I'm going to miss you, Art," she said.

"You come back soon then," he said and kissed her brow.

Alice was flabbergasted to find herself ushered into first class when she boarded the aircraft. "I don't think I'm supposed to be in here," she said to the pretty young stewardess.

"Sure, you are, Miss Ainsley. Your return journey's been upgraded."

Alice thought of Art and smiled. It was typical of him to be so thoughtful and generous. She was feeling some trepidation about going home to England and particularly returning to Langsmead again. The comfort of her seating arrangement would allow her to get a night's sleep and be prepared for whatever tomorrow might bring.

Chapter 19

It was six o'clock in the morning when the plane touched down at Heathrow and Alice was surprised to see Kate waiting at the arrivals terminal.

Alice gave her a hug. "I'm sorry about the change of flight. It's good of you to come at such an ungodly hour."

"Self-interest, I'm afraid," said Kate. "I need you at Langsmead before the crew arrive this afternoon. You know me. I'm like our Prime Minister. Four hours sleep is enough. Though as for last night..." She stopped mid-sentence with a smile on her face.

As they reached Kate's car Alice reminded her that she had to sign the sale completion papers before leaving London.

"Yes, that's all scheduled in." said Kate. "I'm taking you straight to Maxine's office. You can leave the house keys with me and I'll get Ben to collect them. He's ready to start on your job straight away."

"You've thought of everything as usual!" said Alice with a grin.

"That suntan suits you by the way. You look well," she said as they got into the car.

"You were right about Naples, Kate. It's fabulous."

"Look at you, Ali, flying off on exotic holidays while I'm stuck here working. How times have changed!"

"With all your contacts I'm sure you could go anywhere you wanted."

Kate started up the ignition. "The punters with the megabucks are too old for me, Ali," she said, glancing sideways at Alice and letting out a chuckle. "Who'd give a toss for the private jet, not when it strands you on his tropical island and your hoary Lothario can't get it up."

Later, as they drove along the motorway, Kate quizzed her about the holiday. "How did you get on with Art?"

"I think Art is one of the most genuine people I've ever met. I've been thoroughly spoilt Kate."

Alice was on the point of telling her about Art's bizarre marriage proposal but changed her mind. Kate would have been highly amused but Alice didn't like the idea of him being held up to ridicule. Instead, she described her encounter with Jay, the basketball hero.

"Now he sounds like my kind of guy!" said Kate, pulling up outside the village shop. "I'm putting you up at the Gate House while Maria's away so we need to get you some groceries."

As the car pulled into the drive, Kate glanced at her watch and turned to Alice. "I'll have to get back to town after I've paid off the cleaners, but you'll have a few hours to get some kip before the crew put in an appearance."

Alice was glad that she had been allocated the Gate House because she wasn't quite ready to be living in the big house again. After unpacking her overnight bag she decided she should be over there in readiness for the film crew's arrival.

The drawing room offered a good view of the driveway. She settled down in an armchair by the window and opened the book she was reading on the plane. Almost immediately her eyelids were drooping.

The murmur of voices grew more insistent and Alice opened her eyes. The room was crowded with people dressed in black mourning. The mood was as sombre as were the clothes they wore.

Eleanor stood in front of the fireplace and beside her was a large middle-aged woman dressed in an austerely tailored gown with a high collar that fastened under her chin. Her steel-grey hair was drawn away from her plain, jowly face and pinned into a tight bun on the back of her head.

She and Eleanor turned to the tall, distinguished man who approached them. He took Eleanor's hand in his. "I have come to offer you my condolences, Mrs Henshaw."

"You're very kind, Sir William," said Eleanor.

"The news must have come as a terrible shock to you, as it has in fact been to the whole of the nation," he said. "I've come today to represent the Prime Minister and to offer you his most sincere commiserations at this difficult time.

Eleanor nodded. "That is much appreciated, Sir William."

The woman beside Eleanor cleared her throat pointedly. "May I introduce you to my sister-in-law Miss Maude Henshaw," said Eleanor.

After they had exchanged greetings and other pleasantries, Maude expressed her disbelief at the sinking of the Lusitania.

"It seems inconceivable that a passenger liner could have been torpedoed so close to the coast of Ireland, right on our own shores," she said, indignantly.

"Yes, indeed it is, Miss Henshaw," said Sir William. "You echo the feelings of the government The Admiralty are making a full inquiry as we speak."

"*The Times* said that the Lusitania took only eighteen minutes to sink, taking almost two thousand innocent lives with her. Can that be so?" she asked.

"I'm afraid that's correct, Ma'am," he said. "Amongst that number were one hundred and twenty-three American passengers, some of whom were well-known figures. This catastrophe may well turn the mood of the American public."

Maude took Sir William across the room to meet her other brother Edgar, and as she did so, Eleanor's cousin Martha came swiftly over. With her was a tall, good-looking man with light brown hair.

Eleanor's eyes lit up. "Martha, Declan, I'm so glad you're here!"

"We were waiting for the old battleaxe to leave your side," said Martha.

"Yes, she's been attached to me like a convict's manacle," Eleanor said with a smirk. She turned to the man. "It was wonderful of you to come, Declan, but we must take care with Maude. Those gimlet eyes of hers don't miss anything."

"Maude is under the impression that Declan is my fiancé. I see no reason to gainsay her," Martha said with a grin.

"You're bearing up splendidly, sweetheart," Declan said to Eleanor. "You've clearly made a favourable impression on Sir William."

"He's actually a very nice man. I met him a few years ago, before he became a member of the War Cabinet. Handling Henry's family is the tricky part," she said.

Declan glanced across at them and nodded.

"Edgar and his wife aren't so bad, but unfortunately big sister Maude has them all in her thrall," said Eleanor.

"As soon as the dust settles, I'll invite you to London," Martha said. "You could bring the children, too. Where are they, by the way? I'd love to see them."

"They're up in the nursery with Janet. I'm trying to protect them from any more of Maude's maudlin lectures about their father's untimely but heroic demise," said Eleanor. "Maude is seething with fury that I haven't sent George off to school. She talks to the poor lamb as though he were somehow responsible!"

"Stand by your guns, Eleanor," Martha nodded. "It's inhumane to send away the little mites when they're still in short trousers."

Like a scene from a film, the crowd faded out with only Martha, Declan, and Eleanor left in the room. Martha sat in front of the grand piano. She played a polka whilst Eleanor and Declan danced across the parquet floor, whirling round and round again, faster and faster, until they too dissolved into the ether.

The harsh crunch of truck tyres on the gravel driveway banished these phantoms and heralded the arrival of the film crew. The old-fashioned doorbell chimed loudly and standing outside the front door stood an earnest young man.

"Alice Ainsley?" he said.

Alice nodded. "Yes, that's me."

"I'm Chris, the production manager."

He shook her hand briefly and consulted his clipboard. "We'll start to unload then, if that's all right?"

By now, two huge vans were parked in the driveway, and under Chris's watchful eye, people started hurrying purposefully to and fro, unloading their equipment and installing it in the house. A huge catering truck arrived. It was followed by another carrying a generator that Chris directed to the back of the house.

Alice stood beside him in the driveway when a third truck arrived. She stared at the odd looking contraption it carried. "What's that for?"

"It's a snow-making machine. We'll be shooting the exterior shots first, they're scheduled to start tomorrow," he said.

The whole operation was carried out with swift efficiency and within three hours the crew members had left the premises to find their accommodation. Alice took Chris into the kitchen to make him some tea.

He glanced anxiously at his watch. "The crew will be along shortly."

"In the meantime, why don't you sit down and drink your tea?" she said.

He lit a cigarette and Alice asked him when Felicity and the other actors would arrive.

Chris looked at his clipboard. "Felicity Shaw, arriving Wednesday. We start her scenes first thing Thursday. The other actors will also arrive that day, too."

"Have you worked with Sebastian before?"

"Not for a year or so. He was in editing then. This will be his first time directing."

"Oh, really?"

"Seb's got quite a reputation with the birds." He looked at Alice and grinned. "Better watch yourself."

She shook my head and laughed. "No need. I've already met him."

Alice watched Sebastian on the set and was grudgingly impressed by his professionalism. Off the set she kept out of his way as much as possible. One evening he invited her for a drink at the pub and she told him that she had other things to do.

Maria and Victor treated Alice as an honoured house guest at the Gate House and it was good to see them again. Maria was full of news, particularly concerning the arrival of her new granddaughter. She showed Alice a photograph as they sat together at the kitchen table.

"They call her Marissa and she's my spit image!" she said.

"Yes, she does look like you, Maria," said Alice. "Though, of course, you look much too young to be a grandmother at all!"

"I'm forty-nine years old and the mother of five grown up children and three grandchildren!" she said with pride.

Alice dug into Kate's folder to find her menus list and remembered to remind Maria that the film crew had their own catering arrangements. "You only have to cook dinner for the residents. I've got the numbers here as well as the menus. It's a scaled down version of what we usually serve."

Maria glanced over the menu and grunted. "Residents?"

"Yes. That's the important people who are staying in the house. Kate thought it would be best to keep things simple. You may find life a bit disruptive."

Maria looked confused. "Am I in charge of my own kitchen or not?"

"Of course you are, Maria. I'm sure you'll find a way to adapt these dishes. You can make any changes you like," said Alice.

There was little for Alice to do around the place and whenever the weather permitted she went outside to sketch. One day she decided to paint an oil and went into town to buy some more paints. Maria was very happy with the chocolate-box picture she painted of the Gate House and hung it on her living room wall. She also liked to look at Alice's sketches and was usually a very complimentary critic. However, when Alice showed her the new oil Maria put her head on one side and looked at it uncertainly.

"It's mournful," she said.

Alice glanced at her, impressed by the development of her vocabulary. When she looked at the painting propped up on the kitchen table she understood what Maria meant. Alice had spent three days out in the chilly air painting the view from the top of the west lawn, sitting on that bench where she sat with Julian last summer. The dull, grey weather had reflected her mood as did the muted shades of the painting. Everywhere she went there were reminders of Julian and she never went near that green bedroom. It has been easier to block out the memories while in Florida. Art and Erin had cocooned Alice in their loving care but returning to England exposed her to reality once more.

"You're right, Maria. It is a sombre picture," said Alice. "I'll have to paint something more cheerful."

"You're sombre too, Miss Alice. Not like before," said Maria. "We need Mr Julian to make us cheerful again."

She looked at Alice with such motherly concern that Alice put an arm around her shoulders and gave her a squeeze.

Ben phoned Alice daily with a progress report and once she was satisfied that Maria and Victor were accustomed to their new routine she went to meet him at the house.

"We should have finished the plastering by the end of next week," he said, walking with her around the empty rooms.

When Alice arrived his workmates were packing up for the day. The rubble lay in a skip on the roadside and the site was remarkably tidy.

"Tomorrow I'll be in with the plumber and we'll make a start on the bathroom," said Ben.

"I can't believe how much you've done in such a short time," said Alice.

The guys have put in some overtime and we've worked over the weekends. They're always glad of the extra cash," he said. "And you'll be pleased to hear the BT people arrived and installed your telephone this morning."

Alice smiled. "Efficiency must run in the family. Thank you, Ben."

"Don't forget that Stella is expecting you for supper. Come along when you're ready," he said, climbing out of his overalls

The smart new bathroom and kitchen fittings were in their designated places and ready for installation and Alice felt so elated by Ben's progress that she phoned Kate to tell her. Kate was unavailable and on an impulse, she dialled her mother in South Africa. Usually they talked once a month, but it was now almost two since they last communicated.

"Darling, what a lovely surprise!" came her mother Naomi's voice. "I wanted to phone you but didn't know whether you were back from Florida. But guess what, I'm coming back next month. We'll have a lot to catch up on."

"That's great news, Mother. Is Marcus coming with you?"

Naomi hesitated a moment. "No, dear, he won't." She changed the subject. "Did I tell you that John's retiring? You remember John, don't you? He's been managing your grandfather's Yorkshire properties for years now so I'm going to have to make alternative arrangements. I haven't decided yet but I may even sell up. One thing I can tell you is that there are going to be lots of changes. I'll explain it all when I get to London."

There was something going on that she wasn't ready to talk about and Alice suspected it involved Marcus, her fourth husband. He was only ten years Alice's senior and their relationship had never been easy. On her infrequent visits to Cape Town her step-father's business associates often came to the house. They were friendly and charming, but there was something about them she didn't trust, and from the discussions she overheard it appeared that their business deals were as shady as they were.

"You're not thinking of selling Grandma's house I hope," said Alice.

"No, no, dear. The house is owned by the trust," said Naomi. "Why do you ask?"

"Because I love that house," said Alice.

Throughout her fractured adolescence Alice's grandmother Irene had always been there for her, the one constant in her life. Her grandmother's lovely house in Primrose Hill was now rented out but once it had been a haven, the home she returned to during holidays from boarding school and the place where she spent time with her mother during her sporadic visits to England.

Alice remembered vividly the warmth of the friends and relatives who attended her grandmother's funeral in Yorkshire. Alice's great-grandfather had been the overseer of the local coal mine and his only daughter Irene had married the son of her father's boss. The family that she married into were one of the wealthiest in the county, and though she moved with her new husband to London, Irene never lost touch with her roots.

"Well, I look forward to seeing you, darling. It'll be so nice to have some mother-daughter tête-à-têtes again, won't it?" said her mother.

It was now almost two weeks since Alice's return from Florida. She had written to thank Art for his hospitality but they hadn't yet spoken on the telephone. When she dialled his Florida number Erin answered.

"This must be telepathy," she said. "I'm here for a few days to see Dad. I've been trying to reach you at Langsmead because I'm coming to London next week."

"Are you flat hunting already?" asked Alice.

"No, not on this trip," said Erin. She sounded excited. "This is personal stuff. I've got a lot to tell you."

Chapter 20

Alice stayed the night in Ben's flat and the following morning she went to keep an appointment with her doctor in Richmond. Dr Morrison had been her GP for several years and knew her personal as well as her medical history. He confirmed Alice's suspicions.

"Will the father be pleased?" he asked.

"He won't be involved, Dr Morrison," she said. Alice took a deep breath. "I'm going to be a single parent."

He made no comment and continued jotting notes on a pad.

He looked up at her in his kindly paternal manner. "Your mother lives in South Africa, doesn't she?"

"Yes. Cape Town."

"Might you consider having the baby over there?"

"Why?"

"To have your mother at hand."

Alice nodded, smiling wryly, thinking of her mother's mortification at the appearance of a grandchild in her stylish Cape Town home. Having taken advantage of the skills of the country's excellent plastic surgeons she looked more like Alice's sister than mother. The advent of a grandchild would not enhance that image.

"She's coming over here soon," she said.

"I'm glad to hear that, Alice," he said. "You'll need someone to support you."

Alice was both shocked and very excited. After she left the surgery she retraced her steps along the high street and passed a shop she hadn't noticed before. There were some very appealing baby clothes displayed in the window and Alice fought the urge to go inside. Instead, she walked back to where her car was parked by Richmond Green. She was reaching into her bag for the key when she spotted a familiar figure coming out of the adjacent pub. She quickly turned around and fumbled with the key.

"Alice!" Richard called out and she turned to face him.

He came up beside her on the pavement and put a hand on her arm. "I thought it was you, what a marvellous surprise!"

"Hi, Richard, how are you?"

"I'm pretty good, actually, but how are you? It's so great to see you," he enthused. "Look, come and have a drink and let's catch up."

Alice hesitated. "I don't have much time."

"Just a quick one, I insist," he said.

Alice followed him into the pub he had just vacated. It was one they both knew well. Alice sat down at a table and watched him stride across to the bar. He had a deep suntan that emphasised the blue of his eyes, but the lines in his face were more etched than before and his hairline was receding. He was looking his age.

"Here we are then, one sparkling water with lemon and ice," he said, putting down a glass in front of her. "I still can't believe meeting you in the street like that!" he said, taking a seat opposite. "What a bit of luck…"

Alice took a long drink. "So what are you up to these days?"

"I'm making commercials again, working for Ambrose Productions," he said. "I've just come back from a shoot in Bermuda."

"That's great."

"Yes. I finally got my act together," he said with a rueful smile. "It's certainly good to be solvent again."

Alice knew how well commercials paid and nodded. "So how's Priscilla?"

"Oh God, Priscilla!" he exclaimed theatrically, raising a hand to his brow. "She finally went back to her husband."

Alice raised her eyebrows. "Really?"

"Oh, my God Alice. That was such a terrible mistake. Not a day goes by when I don't regret our break-up."

"I've moved on, as they say, Richard."

He made one of those hurt little boy expressions that was once so hard to resist but now left her cold.

"Are you still living around here?" she said conversationally.

"Yes, I've got a flat on Richmond Hill with views across the river. You really must come and see it," he said. "It was a bit of luck actually. The flat belongs to a friend of mine and he's working abroad for a year. By the time he gets back I should be in a position to get my own pad."

"Well, that's all very good news," she said, glancing at her watch. "I really must get going."

"But you haven't told me what you're doing here. I heard you were down in the country with Kate."

"I've just been to see Dr Morrison," I said.

"Nothing wrong, I hope?"

"No, I'm very well indeed. I'm pregnant."

"Oh my God, I thought there was a special glow about you. Congratulations!"

Alice had not intended to impart her news to anyone until a much later date and didn't know why she confided in him. However, sharing her news with someone had turned it into a reality.

"Thank you, Richard," she said, smiling. "Oh, there's one thing I'd like to ask you before I go. Do you know someone called Sebastian Seth-Smith? He's directing a film they're shooting at Langsmead, the house where I'm staying."

Richard nodded. "Yes. He was once a runner at the Beeb. He went by the name Stephen Smith in those days."

Alice chuckled. "Quite a poseur then!"

Richard smiled. "I only saw him a few months ago. I had no idea he was directing. I can tell you one thing about that guy. He really knows how to schmooze."

Richard accompanied her out to her car. "You have a new confidence, Ali. It suits you," he said as he opened the car door. "Good luck, Ali."

No sooner had her car turned into the driveway than Maria came bustling out of the Gate House. "Ah, Miss Alice, I'm so happy you're back."

She followed Alice round to the back of the house and when they arrived in the kitchen, Alice put down her bag and turned to her. "So what's up, Maria?"

"It's these people here, they have no respect!" she said.

Alice sat down at the table. "Whatever have they done?"

"I tell them to wipe their feet, they look at me like I'm foreign rubbish. Mr Sebastian's a proper English gentleman and Madame Felicity, she is a nice lady, but those others are pigs! Either they go or I go – and Victor comes with me."

By now Victor had entered the kitchen. He hovered nearby, clearly discomfited by Maria's tirade.

"Well I'm sorry to hear about all this. I'll have a word with them," she said.

Maria's eyes flashed with anger. "They steal from my fridge!"

"They took Maria's dishes without her permission," said Victor.

When Alice went to find Jeff, the head of the catering staff, he explained that Felicity had been given the aubergine dish for her lunch. "Though when I went to the fridge, I also took out the salmon soufflé," he confessed. "I should have consulted Maria first, but it was the first day Felicity was here and she's very particular about what she eats."

Soon afterwards, Felicity appeared in the kitchen. She was dressed for her film role and looked majestic in an exquisite nineteenth-century ball gown with full stage make-up. Maria stared in awe.

"My dear Maria, how can I make amends for my thoughtlessness?" Felicity's husky voice was at its most caressing. "I never came to thank you for that delicious salmon soufflé. It was the best I've ever tasted and as for the aubergine dish, I have never in my life tasted anything so good."

Maria regarded Felicity as though she was royalty. For a moment Alice thought her bow of obeisance would turn into a full curtsy.

Felicity continued her speech. "It's disgraceful that nobody mentioned that food was removed from your fridge, but it was done at my request. Your cooking is so sublime that I can't resist it. I take full responsibility for what has happened and cannot apologise enough," she said in a tone of exaggerated self-deprecation.

Maria's cheeks flushed deep crimson. "No, no, my lady, it's not your fault. I'm honoured you enjoy my soufflé. It's no problem."

Alice smiled to herself. It was an impressive performance.

With the crisis now over Alice went to watch Felicity perform for the camera. She went to stand beside Chris in the grand hall. "One of her most dramatic scenes," he whispered in her ear.

The clapper boy called out: "Take 2".

It was Eleanor who Alice saw enter the room. She was dressed in an enveloping deep-pink cloak as she entered from the vestibule and walked across the room.

The house was oddly silent. Eleanor looked around. "Hello! I'm home."

She slipped off her cloak, revealing the large protuberance below her bodice, tossed the cloak on a chair then turned in surprise to see Maude standing a few feet away. "Good day to you, Maude. Is this a social visit?" said Eleanor.

Maude stared at her stonily. "So the housekeeper was correct. You are with child."

"Yes, Maude. I am shortly to be a mother again."

"Have you no shame?"

"Shame, Maude?"

"To bring a bastard into the world!" said Maude.

"My fiancé Declan Hathaway is serving his country in France. He is working in a field hospital taking care of our wounded and we would have been married months ago had it not been for the war dragging on as it has. We have had to postpone our wedding until his return."

"Gentlemen don't marry their whores!"

Eleanor's temper was rising and she held onto the banister for support. "What would you know of love, you dried-up old harridan?"

The moment the words were out Eleanor regretted them. It wasn't wise to alienate this embittered woman. She felt her baby stir and put a protective hand on her belly. She took a deep breath. "I think you should know Maude that when Declan returns I shall be leaving this house and taking the children to live with him in London. I will give your brother our address when that happens."

Maude looked at her with an expression close to a sneer.

"And now I'd like you to leave, Maude."

Maude stood immobile. It was then that Eleanor noticed Janet appear behind Maude. Suddenly, everything seemed wrong. Why was Janet's face so red and swollen and why was Maude holding Emily's doll, the doll that never left the child's side?

"What are you doing with that doll, Maude?"

For a brief moment her expression betrayed a flicker of emotion. "I gave this doll to Emily on her last birthday," said Maude.

"Yes, yes. I know that," said Eleanor impatiently. Her heart had started to race. "For God's sake, Maude, tell me why you're here? What's going on?"

Janet stepped forward. She couldn't contain herself any longer. "Oh, Ma'am, oh, Ma'am. There's been an accident."

Eleanor's hand flew to her chest. "The children?"

Maude nodded. "Yes. The same fate has befallen the children as it did their poor Papa."

"What are you talking about, Maude? Is this some cruel joke?" She was now shouting hysterically.

"It happened yesterday afternoon, Ma'am," said Janet with a sob. "They got drowned. They drowned in the lake."

Eleanor stared at her in disbelief. "No! No!"

"They dredged the lake this morning and recovered their little bodies," Janet said in a whisper.

"If you wish to see them the corpses are laid out in the chapel," said Maude.

Janet caught hold of Eleanor as she fainted.

"Cut!"

"That was very good, Felicity, excellent. We'll do the next scene first thing in the morning," said Sebastian.

Alice felt a hand on her sleeve. Chris was staring at her. "It's not for real, you know" he said with one of his rare smiles.

Alice stared at Felicity walking past and brushing away the fake snowflakes attached to her shoulder. Afterwards Alice went into the kitchen to get a drink of water and suddenly Kate appeared through the back door.

"Kate, you're back again?" said Alice.

Kate laughed. "Just couldn't stay away any longer."

Kate had been a regular visitor on the film set and by now her affair with Sebastian was an open secret with the crew. Alice didn't see much of her until the next morning when they had breakfast together on the terrace. Filming was in progress in the Grand Hall, but it was quiet where they sat and the weather was unseasonably warm.

"Seb tells me that the filming is going well and they're even on schedule," said Kate.

"Yes. The only crisis we've had was off set," said Alice and related the incident about Maria and the catering staff.

"Now Felicity has Maria eating out of her hand and the whole crew are treating her with exaggerated deference. Maria is lapping it up!" said Alice with a grin.

Kate laughed and picked up the coffee jug. "Not for me, thanks," said Alice, pointing at the small tea pot beside her.

Kate looked surprised. "No coffee?"

Alice didn't mention that coffee made her feel nauseous. "I prefer tea these days," she said.

Kate knew of Alice's penchant for coffee, particularly at breakfast. She looked at her quizzically. "Are you ill?"

"No…" Alice hesitated a moment. "I'm pregnant."

"You're what?"

Alice nodded. "It was confirmed by Dr Morrison yesterday."

Kate put down her coffee cup. "Good God! Are you saying that you plan to have this baby?"

"Yes."

Kate stared at Alice for a moment, her expression inscrutable. "I see. Well, congratulations, Ali."

That evening Kate went out with Sebastian and Alice didn't see her again until she was about to leave early the next morning. She was chatting to Maria in the kitchen when Kate popped her head around the door. "Well done, Maria. You're doing a splendid job. Must dash now. See you later."

Alice called out goodbye and Kate gave a quick wave.

Kate made another appearance the following week but the visit was brief. Once again Alice saw little of her, but she was so wrapped up in her pregnancy that she didn't miss the absence of their intimate chats. It didn't occur to Alice that Kate might be avoiding her.

Chapter 21

It was the day prior to the end of shooting that Alice received a phone call from Erin. "I got into Heathrow early this morning. Can I come and see you?" she asked.

"I could meet you in town," said Alice. "The crew will be packing up tomorrow."

"I'd prefer to meet you there, if it's okay."

The film crew were dismantling their equipment when Erin arrived. "Is there somewhere quiet we can go? I've got something to show you," she said.

As they went into the library, Erin turned to Alice. "Dad says to say Hi. And by the way, he never stops talking about you. You made a real hit there!"

"How is he?"

"Dad's doing okay," said Erin. "Looks like he may be getting on the political bandwagon, after all."

Alice smiled. "So he's not yet running for Governor of Florida?"

Erin laughed. "I'm working on it!"

She spread a document across the snooker table. "Just look at this, Alice, I've found their records!"

"Whose records?"

"Mom's family tree. Look, this is Herbert and Janet Nicholson, Mom's grandparents.

She took a piece of paper from her folder. "And just take a look at this!"

Alice stared at the photocopy of a marriage certificate. "Oh, good heavens! They were married in the parish of Palehurst. That's only five miles from here!"

"Yes, I remembered the name. That's the place where we went for a swim that day. Isn't it amazing?"

Alice was now as excited as Erin. "I've met someone who might know something about them. She lives in the village."

Alice telephoned Miss Henshaw directly and she invited them over.

As Miss Henshaw led them into her sitting room she turned to Alice with a smile. "Now that we are becoming better acquainted I should like us to be on Christian name terms. Please call me Ellen."

While they drank their tea, Erin explained her mission.

"Herbert and Janet Nicholson, did you say? Yes, let me think. I have a good memory for names, you know," said Ellen. She paused for a moment. "Ah, I remember now, Aggie told me about a girl called Janet who used to work at the house. Janet Jones she was then. Aggie told me about this young man Herbert Nicholson who came courting Janet. He was a good sort, by all accounts, but Aggie was upset when Janet married him because she left so suddenly and Aggie never saw her again. Janet had taken Aggie under her wing when she first arrived at the house and Aggie thought they would become friends, but Janet left without saying goodbye."

Erin could hardly contain her excitement. "So Janet was one of the servants?"

"She was nursemaid to the children," said Ellen. "According to Agnes, Janet wasn't on duty on the day they died. It was her afternoon off and one of the other maids had taken them to the lake. The day that Maude arrived that poor girl was dismissed."

"Just think of that! My great-grandmother worked in the house where I was so recently a privileged guest!" said Erin in amazement. She turned to Ellen. "Did you know that Janet and her husband emigrated to America?"

Ellen shook her head. "No, I had no idea."

"When Janet and Herbert arrived in America, they registered a daughter called Lydia," said Erin. "Their two sons were born on American soil."

"We could go and see whether we can find Lydia in the parish records," said Alice.

"I'd be interested to hear what you discover," said Ellen as we left. "Please keep in touch."

This was when the trail went cold. Though they searched the Palehurst registers as well as all the outlying parishes, there was no record of Lydia Nicholson.

On the evening before Erin returned to America they had dinner together at a London bistro. "Well I don't know what Mom's take will be on all this," said Erin.

"Have you told her about it?" asked Alice.

"No, not yet. You see, Mom's so secretive. Like I said before, she's often talked about her mother with great fondness. but she's kept mute about the rest of the relatives. She didn't even mention that she had an older brother!"

"She must have her reasons."

"Hmm. Like they come from the wrong side of the tracks would be my guess!"

Alice smiled ruefully. "Your Mom and mine seem to have a lot in common."

"Like playing it close to their chest, yeah, that's for sure. Could be a generation thing."

"Seriously, don't you think your Mom will be thrilled to know about Lydia?" said Alice.

"Oh, she'd be thrilled to have me dig up some British aristocrats. I doubt she'll be impressed to know that her grandmother was once a servant!"

The day after Erin left Alice went to see Tom and Poppy. She had been to a tile shop in Fulham recommended by Ben and was just driving away when, on an impulse, she headed towards Knightsbridge. She parked her car in front of a terraced row of smart Georgian houses and checked the house number in her Filofax. She glanced at her watch. By now Tom and Poppy should be back from school.

Felicity greeted Alice effusively at the front door. "Let me show you around the house. It's just been refurbished."

The spacious living rooms had high ceilings and tall sash windows hung with exquisite silk curtains that complimented the elegant period furnishings. Its presentation was as immaculate as Felicity's well-groomed appearance and there was no sign of the clutter usually associated with two energetic young children. When Alice commented on it, Felicity explained that Poppy and Tom had their own quarters upstairs.

The tour had taken at least twenty minutes and as impatient as Alice had been to see Tom and Poppy, she was now feeling drained. "I'll come back to see the children at a more convenient time," she said.

"Oh no," Felicity said. "They'd never forgive me. Come this way."

The kitchen might have leapt straight from the pages of *House and Garden* though its image would not have included the two squabbling children throwing bread pellets at each other across the breakfast table. Poppy's aim missed its target and hit the young Filipino maid who happened to walk past with a basket of laundry.

"What on earth do you think you're doing, Poppy?" asked Felicity crossly. "Apologise immediately."

Poppy turned to the maid. "I'm sorry, Sofia."

Felicity glanced at the breadcrumbs scattered across the polished tiled floor. "And where in heaven's name is Becky?"

"On the phone to her boyfriend," said Tom with a smirk.

Felicity raised her eyebrows and glanced at Alice. "Becky's the new nanny. I don't think she's going to last long!"

Suddenly, Poppy caught sight of Alice and shrieked out her name. Both children ran across the room to her.

Tom was the first to squirm out of Alice's embrace. "I'm so glad you've come, Alice. Now Mum can get rid of that dopey girl."

"Alice is just here to visit us, Tom," said Felicity and went across the room to talk to Sofia.

"And just look at you both!" said Alice, exclaiming at their smart school uniforms. "You look so grown up! I'd hardly have recognised you!"

"Mummy said we'd shot up so much that we had to get lots and lots of new stuff," said Poppy.

"I've got some new football boots and I'm playing in the team next week," Tom boasted, proudly. "Julian says he's coming to watch me. Will you come, too, Alice?"

Poppy was bursting with her own news. "And I've got the best part in the school musical. I'm going to play Annie!"

Alice sat at the table, listening to the excited chatter of school and new friends. Their summer at Langsmead was already a fading memory.

When she finally got up to leave, Poppy pulled on to her sleeve. "You will come again soon, won't you Alice? I've missed you."

"Yes, my poppet. Of course I will," she said, kissing her cheek.

Felicity accompanied Alice back to the front door. "The children have talked about you incessantly, you know."

"I'm very fond of them. They're wonderful children, Felicity," said Alice.

"Then how about you taking over from Becky?" said Felicity with an ingratiating smile.

It took Alice a moment to realise that she was being offered the nanny's job. Alice stared at Felicity in surprise.

"I'd pay you a top salary," she said.

Alice summoned up her haughtiest voice. "Felicity, I'm not a career nanny."

Felicity looked disconcerted. "Oh no, no. It's just that when I saw you at Langsmead I thought you might be at a loose end."

"Oh, no. I've been waiting for the builders to finish so that I can move into my new home," said Alice. "I'll invite the children over once I'm settled in."

At last Ben agreed that the house was habitable and on one very wet Monday in December Alice moved in.

There's still a lot of snagging to be done, so you haven't seen the last of us yet," he told her.

Alice promised that she would work around them and try not to get in the way. She felt she had stayed with Ben and Stella for long enough. Stella offered to come over in her free time and was always ready with a helping hand.

She went with Alice to choose the paint and insisted that she was a dab hand with a paint brush. Alice enjoyed having her around. She had spent a very intense week with Erin and afterwards she missed her company.

Alice hadn't seen Kate for weeks and was pleased when one day she appeared at her front door unexpectedly. It was just as Stella was about to leave. They had been painting the spare bedroom and Stella was dressed in overalls with her hair tucked into a scarf that was tied in the style of a 1940s land girl. Alice thought the look suited her very well.

As Stella came into the hallway Alice said to Kate. "You remember Stella."

Kate stared at her blankly. "Stella, Ben's girlfriend," said Alice.

"Oh, yes. Hallo there," said Kate.

With a quick peck on Alice's cheek Stella hurried off through the doorway. Alice took Kate into the living room.

"Do I know her?" asked Kate.

"Yes, of course you do, Kate. Ben brought her to meet you at the hotel. I came with them."

"Oh, that one!"

"Ben is crazy about her. They're really good together."

"You don't think it's serious, do you?"

"It certainly is. Stella moved in with him three months ago."

"What, that hippy!"

"Stella isn't a hippy, Kate. She just dresses the way she feels comfortable."

"Well, I don't know why Ben hasn't told me."

Alice was beginning to feel irritated. "Would you like a glass of wine, Kate?"

"Yes, please," she said and followed Alice out to the kitchen. "You must admit, Ali, she is—"

Alice cut her off. "Kate, Stella is a lovely person and great for Ben. She's become a good friend and I'm very fond of her."

After Kate sat down with her wine in the living room she was more subdued than usual. She hadn't seen Alice's house before and apart from a polite 'It's very nice' she made no comment and didn't ask to look around.

"It's good to see you again, Kate. How are you?" said Alice.

"Not so bad. And you?"

Alice patted the bulge under my jumper. "I'm very well and the baby is doing well, too."

"Ah, yes. The pregnancy."

For a few minutes Alice talked about the excellent care she was receiving at the ante-natal clinic.

Kate sipped her wine and lit a cigarette. Alice stared at her for a moment thinking how like a stranger she was. Where had the old intimacy between them gone?

"How is Sebastian?" asked Alice.

"Oh Seb, he's good. Busy working on the editing at the moment," said Kate.

"Are you serious about him?"

"Seb worships the ground I walk on!" she said with a laugh. "And oh, what a stud! He can't get enough of it. Do you know, when he wants sex, and that is pretty often, he tells me that he wants to brush my hair! Once we did it in the housekeeper's linen cupboard and nearly got rumbled." She chuckled to herself. "The risk factor gives sex another dimension, you know."

Alice laughed. "Yes. It must make you feel like a teenager again."

Alice couldn't help wondering whether sex was all this relationship was about because after these revelations Kate spoke no more of him and was silent for such a long time that Alice rummaged around for another topic. "I went to see Tom and Poppy a couple of weeks ago and Felicity offered me the nanny's job!"

Kate raised her eyebrows and took a deep draw on her cigarette. "Fancy that!"

Alice topped up Kate's wine glass. "That's a really beautiful house she has."

"Did you know that Julian was moving in?"

"What! Julian is going to live with Felicity?"

"She mentioned it when she came over to the hotel the other day. I said she'd get him once I was no longer on the scene."

Alice didn't recall Kate saying exactly that but let it go.

"What I've only just realised is the game they've been playing. I could kick myself for that."

"What do you mean, Kate?"

"It's obviously been going on for a long time, well before she and Tim split up."

Alice stared at her in disbelief. "Why do you say that?"

"I must have told you how they were always on the phone to each other last summer. And look at the way they dumped those kids on me. I was just the stooge. They used me, Alice."

Alice's head was spinning. What was it he said that day by the lake? 'You can think you know someone really well and feel very close to them and then you discover you don't know them at all. It happens more often than you'd think.' Was that a warning she should have paid heed to?

"Well, hey ho! Life can be a bummer," said Kate. "Well, I'd best be going. Got to get back."

Kate drank up her wine, brushed a kiss across Alice's cheek and departed.

Chapter 22

By the time her mother's plane landed at Heathrow Alice's house was looking good. The wood floors had been sanded and polished. The curtains were hung and the spare bedroom was ready.

"I've booked myself into Kate's hotel. I hope it's as comfortable as on my last visit," said Naomi as they walked towards the car park.

"You look tired, Mum," she said. Alice was disturbed by her appearance. Her mother was so pale and drawn and there were fine grey strands in her dark brown hair that Alice had never seen before. Even her deep blue eyes lacked their usual lustre.

As Alice drove along the Brompton Road they passed by Harrods and her mother looked out of the car window excitedly. It was two weeks before Christmas and the department store's windows were ablaze with sparkling fairy-tale displays. "You know, that's something I always missed in South Africa. There's nothing like Christmas in England," she said.

"You know, Mum, my house is in good shape now if you want to come and stay," she said.

"Yes, dear, that sounds very nice," said Naomi. "Perhaps I'll come for a few days though I don't want to put you out, have you bothered with lots of cooking and so on. Still, we could always eat out."

"But I'd like to."

"Well, if you're sure you're up to it."

"Yes, of course I am. I'm pregnant, Mum, not ill. Apart from a bit of nausea in the morning, I've never felt better."

"Good. Then why not come up to Yorkshire with me?" she said. "I have to go there on business."

Alice hadn't visited Yorkshire since her grandmother's funeral. Immediately she agreed.

While her mother was attending to her business affairs, Alice paid several visits to her grandmother's grave, sitting on the grass at the foot of the tombstone and telling her about the baby and her new home. On the last day of their visit Alice went to say goodbye to her and was just getting up from the ground when she heard someone behind me.

"I thought I would find you here," said Naomi.

For a few minutes they stood together in silence and then Naomi put a hand on Alice's shoulder. "Come on, darling. it's time to go and catch that train."

They didn't speak again until they were settled into the first-class compartment of which they were the only occupants. After the train moved out of the station, Naomi looked across at Alice sitting opposite. "I know how hard it was for you. I've been an appalling mother."

Alice looked up from the magazine she was reading. It was unlike her mother to speak with such candour. "In many ways, you're so like your grandmother. I was always grateful you had her in your life," she said.

Alice put down the magazine. "Okay, Mum. What's all this about?"

"I suppose it's about me. I never appreciated my mother enough while she was alive."

"And now you feel regret?"

Naomi nodded. "You see, everything at home changed after Jamie died. In no way could I compensate for my parents' loss. I never felt I was good enough."

Alice had seen photographs of her mother's elder brother in her grandmother's house and knew his history. Jamie had died soon after his eighteenth birthday; he had an accident while out riding his friend's motor bike.

"Your grandfather didn't approve of the set Jamie got in with and forbade him to see them, but Jamie disobeyed. A light went out in my parents' life. My mother immersed herself in the work of the many charities she ran, but my father lost his zest for life. As you know, he was a fine architect, acclaimed for his Festival of Britain designs. He lost interest in his business and worked at home on a few pet projects leaving Godfrey, his junior partner, to take over the day-to-day running of the company. Godfrey came to the house regularly to discuss the company's various projects. That is how I met him."

"My father? Hmm, I don't remember him very well."

"No. He was ill for a long time and you can't have been more than five or six when he died."

"What was he like?"

"Godfrey was a kind, shy man, in his late thirties when we first met. When he started coming round to the house he developed a crush on me. I was flattered by his attention and often played up to it. I was seventeen and stuck at home under my father's watchful eye. When my mother realised how trapped I felt she suggested a year at a French finishing school. I jumped at the chance to escape."

"And when you came back you and Godfrey got married?"

She shrugged. "Ah, that's another story."

Alice stared at her, wondering. There was something here that didn't add up, a piece was missing from the puzzle.

"I remember the day you dropped me at Grandma's and bolted. We didn't see you again for months," said Alice.

"I know I can never make amends for your lonely childhood, but I want you to know that I've always been so proud of you, Alice. Now at last we have the chance to really get to know each other. That's something I've longed for."

Alice stared through the window at the back gardens of the suburbs whizzing by. "Are you going to tell me about you and Marcus?"

"It's over between us. Marcus was too young for me."

"He always was. What's changed?"

"Marcus went into business with a dubious crowd whom I regarded as the Cape Town Mafia. I told him I'd leave him if he didn't give up his association with them, however many millions he expected to make. He didn't." She gave a rueful smile. "Grandma always said I had bad taste in men!"

Alice grinned. "That's something we have in common!"

She had many other questions to ask of her mother but she looked so dejected that Alice decided to wait.

When her mother phoned two days later, her voice was much more upbeat. "Look, darling, I won't be able to see you this evening," she said. "I'm going to the theatre. I hope you don't mind."

Alice didn't tell her that she had already started preparing the meal for their supper together.

"I'll make it up to you tomorrow. Could you be at the hotel at ten?" she said. "I have a little surprise in store."

Richard arrived on Alice's doorstep early next morning. She had only been up for a few minutes and went to open the front door in her dressing gown.

Two weeks had passed since his first visit. It was the afternoon that she had taken delivery of the new furniture and she had been staring uncomprehendingly at the assembly instructions for the bookcase when the doorbell rang. Hoping that by some miracle the delivery man had returned, she ran to the door. It had been a shock to find Richard standing on her doorstep, but after a moment's hesitation she invited him in.

Planks of wood were strewn across the living room floor and she had explained her dilemma, thrusting the instructions into his hand.

"I can put this up for you, Ali. No problem at all. I'm working today, but as soon as I have a free moment I'll be back," he'd said, tidying the planks into a neat pile.

Alice had put Richard's visit out of her mind and was surprised to see him again. "What are you doing here, Richard?" she asked.

"I've come to put up that bookcase, Ali. I said I'd come when I had a free day."

She pulled in the tie of her dressing gown. "Oh, the bookcase. I see. Well, you'd better come in."

Richard ran his eye over the diagram. "Looks easy enough. I'll have this up in a trice."

"I'm afraid I'll have to leave you to it. I've got to go out."

"That's fine, Ali. Just show me where you want it."

Alice left him to assemble the bookcase and as she went upstairs for a shower she realised it might have been wiser to have sent him away.

"How did you find my address in the first place, Richard?" she asked him when she came back downstairs.

"Kate."

"Kate gave you my address?"

"Yes. I bumped into her weeks ago. She was with that guy Sebastian as he calls himself now."

"Oh."

He turned to her with a grin. "Actually he's not such a bad bloke. Looks like he's going places."

"Really?"

"I thought he and Kate were an item."

"Yes. I believe they are."

"Well, he was with a stunning young Asian girl at the Ivy the other day and she was with him again at a party two days later. Perhaps it's best not to mention it to Kate."

"I shan't."

"Next week we're meeting up to discuss a project I have in mind. He's got really useful contacts."

"Ah, so it's strictly business, is it?"

He smiled. "Yes, Ali. Strictly business!"

Naomi appeared from the lIft in a waft of Channel. "Look darling, could we just have a word?" she asked, rearranging the glamorous fur coat that was draped around her shoulders. "I have a favour to ask you."

"So, what can I do for you, Mum?" asked Alice.

She looked at Alice sheepishly. "Would you mind if I invited a friend to join us for Christmas dinner?"

"Not at all," Alice nodded. "Who is it?"

"Oliver Selby. He's a friend from way back. Oliver's a widower now."

Alice smiled. "Is Oliver the mystery theatre date, by any chance?"

Her mother smiled coyly and nodded. "If you don't mind, I'd like to go and give him a ring. I didn't want to say anything until I had spoken to you."

"Of course not," said Alice. "Go on, off you go."

Alice watched her disappear into the lift and noticed Kate talking to the concierge. She waved and called out to her.

"This is a surprise," said Kate, coming over. "What are you doing here?"

"I've come to meet my mother. She's just gone to make a phone call," said Alice.

"Would you like some coffee while you're waiting?" Kate asked in the efficient manner she usually reserved for guests.

She called a waiter over and turned to leave.

"Kate, don't go," said Alice. "I've been trying to get you on the phone, but you don't return my calls."

"Oh, sorry. Just busy, you know. Up to my eyes!"

"Kate, why did you give Richard my address?"

She looked nonplussed for a moment. "Oh, he was so desperate to have it. He was with Seb at the time. They may be going into business together, you see."

"So it was strictly business then?"

"That's right, babe, strictly business."

For a moment Alice wanted to laugh but this was Kate, her friend.

Once Naomi was settled in the back of the taxi she turned to Alice. "Is something the matter? You look upset."

Alice shook her head. "It's nothing."

Naomi sat forward and knocked on the glass screen that separated them from the driver. "This isn't the way to Harrods, young man!"

The driver pushed back the screen and turned his head. "Sorry, Missus but there's road works ahead. There's been a gas leak."

Naomi glanced at her watch in irritation. "We'll be late for the appointment," she tutted and then sat back in her seat. "I had a chat with Kate while I waited for Oliver last night." Something in a shop window caught her eye and she paused for a moment. "What was I saying? Oh, yes, Kate. She's a funny one."

"Why do you say that?"

"She was odd, that's all. I was talking about the baby and saying how excited I was at the prospect of being a grandmother..."

Alice glanced at her. "Are you really, Mum?"

"Yes, Alice, I am. It's a surprise to me, too, darling, but I'm actually thrilled to bits by your news."

"That's nice."

"I think you should know too that I want to be with you for the birth of your baby. You see, I intend to be a hands on grandmother, just as my mother was for you."

Alice smiled. "Thank you, Mum. I'm really happy to hear that."

Naomi smiled back at her and nodded. "Now as I was saying, Kate was in a very odd mood. She had this blank expression on her face, you see. For a moment I thought she was jealous, but then I remembered how adamant she was about not having children. I'm right about that, aren't I?"

Suddenly, the penny dropped. Kate was upset about her pregnancy. What a fool she had been not to realise.

Alice nodded and Naomi said no more. For all her parental shortcomings, Alice acknowledged that her mother had remarkable tact. She never pried too far and had not even questioned her about the baby's paternity. Alice knew her mother would wait until she was ready to tell her.

They got out of the lift at Harrods on the fourth floor and presented themselves at the reception desk. A pretty young blonde woman appeared to be expecting them and led them off into the beauty salon.

Alice glanced at her mother. "What's going on?"

Naomi winked. "Just a little pampering. I thought we could do with it."

Two and a half hours later they emerged from the salon with glowing complexions and perfectly manicured nails. "And now for the hair," said Naomi, ushering Alice towards the hair salon.

A handsome stylist called Luigi greeted her mother like an old friend.

He sat them down and started playing with Naomi's hair. "So this lovely lady is your daughter Alice? I don't believe I've had the pleasure."

He came to stand behind Alice's chair and looked at her in the mirror. "Ah, yes, the same shaped eyes and fine bone structure," he said and turned to pick up a comb.

With her mousey blonde hair and blue-grey eyes Alice often thought she paled into insignificance beside her glamorous mother, but when she looked at the mirror that morning she could see their resemblance for the first time.

Before leaving they passed through men's clothing and Naomi spotted a display of cashmere sweaters. She picked one up in dark blue and held it out.

Alice nodded. "It's lovely."

"Yes, I think this will do nicely," said Naomi and handed it over to the sales assistant. "I'd like it in large, please."

Alice was overwhelmed, not only by the events of that day but also by the quantity of bags that were loaded into the taxi. She had forgotten what it was like to go shopping with her mother.

"We'd like to go to Clapham, please," Naomi instructed the driver. She turned to Alice. "I think it best we take this lot directly home, don't you?"

"That's odd, the lights are all on," said Alice before putting her key into the lock.

"Hi Alice," said Richard, appearing on the other side of the door. He noticed the quantity of bags and came out to help.

The living room lights were dimmed and a Chopin sonata played softly in the background. "This looks very cosy," said Naomi, sitting down on the sofa with a sigh. "All I need now is a nice long gin and tonic."

"Right you are, one gin and tonic coming up," said Alice, going to the doorway where Richard was hovering.

"Let me," he said.

Alice glanced at the bookcase now erected against the living room wall and frowned. "Have you been here all day?"

"No, but I noticed your spare key in the kitchen and just popped back to see to a couple of things. I secured that loose light fitting in the hallway," he said. "Oh, by the way, you had a visitor, Ali."

"Who was that?" she asked.

"A bloke. Tall, dark-haired, in his forties."

"He didn't give his name?"

"No. I introduced myself and invited him in. He said he couldn't stay."

Alice's heart missed a beat. "Oh, my God!" she whispered, turning pale.

Naomi glanced up at her. "Is something the matter, dear?"

"No, no. It's okay," said Alice. She took a deep breath. "Richard, the drinks are in the kitchen, left cabinet by the door, lemons are in the fridge."

"You come and sit down, Alice. It's been a long day," said Naomi, patting the seat beside her. She eyed the empty lager can on the table. "Richard seems to be making himself at home."

"Hmm, making himself useful, too," said Alice.

"He's not the baby's father, is he?" said Naomi.

"Who, Richard? God no!" said Alice.

Naomi let out a sigh of relief. "Thank goodness for that!"

"I told you, we broke up months ago. I met him by chance and then he turned up here unexpectedly."

"Not at your invitation?"

Alice shook her head. "Most definitely not, though I'm afraid I did accept his offer to put up the bookcase. It was a mistake."

"Fine, dear. I just needed to be sure."

"Here we are ladies, two gin and tonics," said Richard, coming back into the room. He handed a glass to Naomi and the other to Alice "Not to worry, Ali, yours is mostly tonic, just a dash of gin."

Naomi glanced at him with eyebrows raised.

He sat down on an armchair and opened a can of lager. "Are you staying long, Naomi?" he asked.

"Yes," she said shortly and took a drink from her glass. She turned to Alice. "Did I tell you that Oliver has recently retired?"

"No. Retired from what?"

"Advertising," said Naomi. "Selby and Bingham. Oliver started the company back in the '60s."

Richard looked impressed and sat forward. "Wow! Selby and Bingham! They're one of the biggest agencies in town."

"You'll find Oliver is a very unassuming man and he's great fun," said Naomi.

"I'll look forward to meeting him," said Alice.

"Well, I'd certainly like to meet the guy," said Richard.

Naomi turned to look at him as though she had forgotten he was there.

"Richard's working in commercials these days," said Alice.

Naomi nodded. "You know, darling, I'm really rather tired. Would it be all right for me to stay here tonight?"

"Of course. The room's all ready for you," said Alice.

She got up and went across to look at the bookcase. Two of the shelves were filled by the books she had left in a box on the floor. She turned to Richard. "The bookcase looks very nice, Richard. Thank you for that."

She had hoped he would take the hint and leave but he got up and came towards her. "Alice, when can we talk?" he asked, quietly.

"Talk about what?" she asked.

"About us," he said.

She stared at him stonily. "There is no us, Richard."

"Look, I know I messed up and gave you a lot of pain, but I've changed. I'm a new man now and I'm earning good money," he said.

Alice put up her hand. "If you're saying what I think you had better stop now, Richard."

"But I could take care of you – and the baby, of course," he said.

Alice stared at him, speechless.

"I don't think Alice needs any support from you Richard, nor from anyone else for that matter," said Naomi.

He turned to her in surprise. "But Naomi—"

"Don't you have a home of your own to go to, Richard?" she said.

He went to the door. "Please think it over, sweetheart. Remember how good it was once."

"Please go," said Alice.

She took Naomi's glass into the kitchen and poured her another drink. When she returned to the living room she sat down on the chair that Richard had just vacated. "Thanks for that, Mum."

Naomi gave a wry smile. "The pleasure is all mine."

Alice took a long drink of her tonic water and kicked off her shoes. "Bloody men! Right now, I could do with a strong drink."

"Don't let Richard get you down, Alice."

"I'm fine, Mum."

"Richard isn't worth it."

"Oh, it's not him. I actually found Richard rather pathetic."

"Your visitor?"

Alice nodded. "Julian. He's the baby's father."

"I see."

Alice was furious that Julian had found Richard in her house. On the other hand, what would she have said to Julian had they met face to face? That had not happened. It would be wiser not to speculate.

She turned to her mother. "Mum, there's something I've been wanting to talk to you about for a long time."

"Yes?"

"It's about Dad," said Alice.

"Go on."

"He wasn't my natural father, was he?"

"Why do you say that?"

"It's a gut feeling, really. But there were lots of little things that I picked up on over the years, particularly when I was eavesdropping on your conversations with Grandma."

"Godfrey was a good man and he loved you as a daughter, but you are quite right. Godfrey wasn't your father."

"Why didn't you tell me?"

"It's difficult to explain, but I know I should have told you a long time ago. You do have a right to know." She took a drink from her glass and put it down on the coffee table. "I met your father John in a Paris art gallery. He was with a group of American postgraduates touring Europe. John was very good looking. You have his colouring."

"He was American?"

"Yes, John was an American."

"What happened?"

"It was the end of my school year and I should have returned home, but John and I had fallen in love. We went together to Arles and stayed in a pension. John was crazy about the Impressionist painters. When our money ran out we had to leave. John had nothing left but his return ticket to the States. He was a working-class boy and his parents had used most of their savings to send him on this trip."

"You must have both been devastated," said Alice.

Naomi nodded. "I waved goodbye at the train station and we never saw each other again."

"Didn't you write?" asked Alice.

"Yes, we did, at first. But, when I wrote to tell him that I was pregnant, I didn't receive a reply. Three months later, just after I married Godfrey, he wrote to tell me his father had died and for financial reasons he and his family had moved to another state to live with his mother's relatives. He never received that letter."

Oliver arrived promptly at noon on Christmas morning. He was armed with prettily wrapped packages and a box of expensive wine. Alice stood beside her mother in the hallway.

Oliver had a twinkle in his eye as he smiled at her. "Oh my, how you've grown, Alice!"

"When you were very small Oliver and Susan, his wife, were close neighbours and we saw a lot of each other." said Naomi.

Alice didn't know whether it was his voice or the merry twinkle in his eye that triggered a memory.

"Oh, yes!" she grinned. "You were the funny man who always made me laugh!"

The years had been kind to Oliver. He was over six foot and like many tall men, he had a slight stoop, but his face was relatively unlined and he had a full head of silver-grey hair.

Naomi, who was watching them with a slight anxious frown, burst into laughter. "Well, what did I tell you, Oliver!" she said. "I knew you two would hit it off."

He looked down at her and smiled. Their mutual affection was palpable.

It was later, after the dishes had been cleared from the dinner table that Alice learned of the length of their friendship.

Oliver glanced across at Alice as he shuffled the cards for a third round of gin rummy. "At seventeen your mother was the belle of the county. She left a trail of broken hearts in her wake," he said with a grin.

"Oh, stop it, Oliver. That's not true at all," said Naomi, smacking his hand playfully.

"Well I should know, shouldn't I?" he said.

Alice laughed. "So you were one of them, were you, Oliver?"

"We did keep in touch though, didn't we?" said Naomi.

"After your mother moved away, we used to exchange Christmas cards," said Oliver. "But last year I didn't receive one and I wrote to her."

"And then you phoned and suggested we meet up again," said Naomi.

"You'd never believe, Alice, how hard it was to get her to agree. Your mother can be very stubborn!" he said.

"But Oliver, after all these years, I was nervous!" Naomi said, indignantly.

"The truth is, Alice, I've been holding a torch for your mother for close to forty years," he said. "The problem for me was that I never managed to catch her between marriages!" He made the statement with such solemnity that it was impossible not to smile.

Naomi was in love again and for the first time Alice approved.

Chapter 23

Alice stood looking at the lakeside painting hanging on the wall over the fireplace. Her mother had told her how she found it tucked away in a cupboard while she was tidying up, knocked a hook into the wall and hung it up. "Look, doesn't it look perfect there?" she said smiling. "Did you paint it, Alice?"

Alice nodded. "Yes. I painted it last summer."

"I didn't know my daughter was so talented," she said smiling.

Alice didn't mention that Kate had sent the painting to her a few days before Christmas, carefully packaged and sent by special courier, nor of the cryptic message attached. Alice didn't understand the message and telephoned Kate several times before finally reaching her.

"I know you're upset, Kate. Couldn't we meet and talk about it?"

"There is no point."

"I don't understand."

"Then you're not as bright as I thought," said Kate.

"What is that supposed to mean?" asked Alice.

"Our friendship is over, Alice. Please don't bother me again."

Thanks to the painting, every day Alice was reminded of Kate and last summer; and when she went to sleep Eleanor was back in her dreams, more present than before. It was now late February and her mother had just departed with Oliver on a Caribbean cruise. Alice lifted down the painting and carried it out to the dustbin but changed her mind halfway there. It ended up stowed away in the back of a cupboard.

When Stella and Ben came over for dinner one evening Stella noticed the blank wall. "Where's that picture, Alice?" she asked.

"Gone. It belongs to the past," said Alice.

She nodded. "Good. Glad to hear it."

They had just finished eating and Alice was in the kitchen preparing the green tea that Stella said was so good for them when she overheard her conversation with Ben.

"Why on earth did Kate do that?" she said.

"What, send the picture back to Alice?" he said.

"Yes. That was a petty thing to do, totally unnecessary."

Ben frowned. Due to his work on the renovations, recently he had seen more of his sister than he had in years. These days there was an edge to her that he hadn't seen when she was younger. "Hmm. Kate's changed," he said. "She's much more brittle than she used to be."

"Or perhaps you never noticed that mean side of her," said Stella. "Your big sister can be one right royal bitch."

Alice was mortified that Kate had decided to end their friendship. She wondered whether she, too, had been blind to Kate's dark side.

Alice attended her ante-natal classes each week without fail. She took great delight in her increasing girth. Judging by the way she was carrying, Stella speculated on her having a boy though Alice herself had no preference; all she cared was that her baby was healthy. As she decorated the nursery she hugged the thought that within twelve weeks her baby would be occupying this room. There were moments when she longed to share her excitement with his father. As soon as she felt confident that the pregnancy would go full term, she had fully intended to tell him but not any more. The news of him moving in with Felicity had made her very angry. She was too hurt to consider having him share the baby's life.

"You don't think the father has a right to know?" her mother asked on the eve of her departure for the cruise.

"No, Mum. Julian is not the man I thought him to be," Alice answered.

"But you're still in love with him, aren't you?" said Naomi.

Alice glanced sharply at her mother. "Why do you say that?"

"Oh, I see that faraway look in your eyes sometimes..."

Alice frowned. "My only concern is the baby now, Mum."

Alice was humming to herself as she painted a mural on the nursery wall. She had chosen a Beatrix Potter theme. As she stepped back to appraise Peter Rabbit, the telephone rang. The call was from Ellen Henshaw to tell her that she had some news that would be of interest to her and to Erin. Alice contacted Erin and they arranged a date to meet Ellen.

Erin and Alex had arrived in England at the end of January and were now living in Canary Wharf, having moved there from what Erin described as 'the poky flat' that Alex's company had found them. The new apartment was a penthouse flat with views over the river. When Alice had first visited her there Erin showed her around the spacious rooms. "This must be costing the company a bomb!" Alice commented.

Erin shook her head. "It's me who wanted this place so I'm going to pay the extra. I'm getting a job."

"A job, Erin?"

"Don't look so surprised, Alice. I'm not some spoilt brat who gets it all handed over on a plate!" she said indignantly. "I've been imbued with Dad's work ethic all my life. Even as a young kid I earned my pocket money by doing the chores Dad thought up for me. And later when I stayed with him in Florida he set me to work on one of his pet charities and that was slave labour!"

Alice laughed. "So what kind of job are you after?"

"I've got an interview at an art gallery in Bruton Street next week. They specialise in British oils so I'm swatting up on the local talent, old and new. I guess I can bluff my way through!"

It was a wintry day in late March when they drove off to keep their rendezvous with Ellen. Alice glanced at Erin sitting behind the wheel of Alex's new car. When Erin had first pointed out the shiny black four-wheel drive parked in the square outside the block of flats, Alice had stared at it dubiously. "Are you certain you can you drive that?"

"Sure, I can," she said with a grin.

Before they pulled out of the parking area Alice questioned her ability to navigate our roads. "Just chill out, will you Alice?" she said.

She drove along the motorway with such assurance that Alice turned to her and grinned. "I won't ever doubt you again, Erin, I promise."

"Did Ellen give you any clue as to what this is all about?" she said.

"No. She just said she had made a discovery and wanted to discuss it in person," said Alice.

Ellen was waiting for them in the restaurant of a small hotel on the outskirts of the village. "It's about Eleanor," she said without preamble as they sat down to lunch.

"Last Sunday I was reading an article about the Fabians in one of the supplements and there were two paragraphs about Martha Farthingale," she said, handing over the magazine. "She was Eleanor's cousin."

The article described Martha's involvement in the Society, particularly her lobbying for a universal healthcare system. It also mentioned her long nursing career, citing instances of her courage and fortitude whilst nursing the wounded in France during the First World War.

"Suddenly I remembered a puzzling incident that happened when I was a child," said Ellen. "A young woman I had never seen before came to visit my parents and the three of them were closeted in the library for ages. Aggie, who was now married to Dave's father, told me that the young woman was Martha Farthingale."

"And you don't know the reason for her visit?" asked Alice.

Ellen shook her head. "All I can tell you is that the young woman was crying when she came out and my parents looked upset. I heard my mother saying that

Maude was a very wicked woman. Aunt Maude was my father's elder sister, but she was never invited to our house again, not even at Christmas."

"It must have been connected to Eleanor," said Alice.

"Yes, and that's what I want to tell you. You see, after reading that article, I searched amongst my father's private files that I've kept boxed up in my study and found one containing his personal correspondence."

After lunch they went back to Ellen's cottage. Ellen opened the folder that lay on the coffee table. She took out a letter and handed it to Erin. "I think you should read this. In the meantime, I will make coffee."

Erin read the letter twice before holding it out to Alice. The letter was dated October, 1940.

Dear Edgar,

As you know I have been concerned regarding the mysterious circumstances surrounding the death of my cousin Eleanor. Accordingly, I hired the services of a private investigator called Mr Frobisher. Your sister Maude was unwilling to talk to Mr Frobisher, but when he interviewed Mrs Jenny Martin, the midwife who attended the confinement, an astonishing fact emerged. When Jenny Martin had last seen them she said that both Eleanor and the baby girl were alive and well.

Afterwards I visited Jenny Martin myself. Jenny said when Maude had employed her services she was sworn to secrecy and paid handsomely to keep her silence. I questioned Jenny at length until finally she recalled an incident that had puzzled her. She said that the day following the birth she had returned to the house to check on her patients. It wasn't an easy birth and the mother had been in a very distressed state. She rallied when the baby was put in her arms and told Jenny that she would call her Lydia, Jenny told me. However, Maude barred Jenny's entrance and told her that her services were no longer required. As she turned to leave Jenny noticed a girl hurrying across the yard and in her arms she carried a bundle covered up in a shawl. Jenny was suspicious and wanted to see the bundle, but the girl had vanished.

Upon making further inquiries I discovered that it was the same day that one of the maids had left her employment at Langsmead to get married and I have ascertained that girl to be Janet Nicholson née Jones.

My family and I believe it imperative that the young couple be apprehended without delay. I should be grateful to have your cooperation in this matter and will be happy to visit you at your convenience.

With kind regards,

Martha

Ellen returned to the room with a coffee tray and set it down on the table. She glanced at Erin and Alice. "Extraordinary, isn't it?" she said. "I wish I'd had the pleasure of meeting Miss Farthingdale."

Erin wiped her eyes on her sleeve and Alice handed her a tissue. "I just can't believe this!"

Ellen sat down. "My guess is that Maude bribed the girl and paid for her and her new husband to emigrate."

Erin nodded "Hush money."

"It can be the only explanation," said Ellen. "There is more correspondence in that folder that relates to their unsuccessful search. After a gap of many years there is another letter dated 1942 that refers to some family heirlooms Martha had packed in a leather trunk after retrieving them from her bombed-out home and asking Edgar whether she might store the trunk at Langsmead."

"That trunk I brought to your house?" said Alice.

Ellen nodded and turned to Erin. "Strictly speaking, I think that trunk and its contents are rightfully yours."

Alice slipped her arm through Erin's as they walked out to the car. "You'll need to make some adjustments to that family tree, Erin."

"Yes, I do," she said "But first my Mom needs to hear this."

Two days later she flew to Boston.

Chapter 24

"Ahm up the duff," said Stella.

Erin looked bemused. "You're what?"

Alice came into the living room and smiled indulgently at the pair of them. Erin had been away for over two weeks and it was good to have her back. Alice was also pleased to see how well her two friends were getting along.

"She means she's pregnant," said Alice.

"You're not, are you Stella?" said Erin.

Stella laughed. "Not blooming likely."

"You had me worried there. For a nanosecond I thought it could be contagious!" said Erin.

"Here's me doing my Eliza Doolittle thing and all you want to hear is ma Geordie!" said Stella.

"But it's such a quaint dialect," said Erin.

It had just gone one o'clock and Alice asked the girls whether they'd like something to eat.

"First there's something I have to tell you, Alice. You'd best sit down," said Erin.

"Do you want me to scram?" said Stella.

"No need," said Erin. She turned to Alice. "It's about your father."

"My father! But he died long ago," said Alice.

"I'm talking about your natural father, John Cummings."

Alice stared at her. "You know something about him?"

"Yes, Alice, I do. Cummings is my mother's maiden name. I thought it was too much of a coincidence so I didn't say anything before checking it out."

"You mean they're related?" said Alice.

"And so are we! John Cummings was my mother's elder brother."

Alice was too astonished to speak.

Erin laughed. "Well, I always wanted a sister, but I guess a cousin will have to do!"

Alice got up to give her a hug and they both started crying.

"Stop this, you two or you'll get me going," said Stella.

Erin sat down beside Alice and took her hand. "Look honey, I'm sorry to say that John Cummings died from cancer fifteen years ago."

Stella went across the room and picked up her bag. "I'm off to the deli to get us summat to eat."

Twenty minutes later she was back, laden with cold meats and salads that she arranged on the coffee table.

"I've made an inventory of the stuff from Martha's trunk," said Erin and put down a typewritten page on the table.

"Blimey! Eighteenth-century cruet sets and nineteenth-century sugar tongs! This stuff is for posh folk!" said Stella, scanning down the list.

She pointed at an item on the page. "What's an embossed silver Vesta when it's at home?"

Erin looked over her shoulder. "That's a Vesta case. It's for keeping matches in. You can use it to light them, too."

Stella rolled her eyes. "Then why can't they write it in plain English!"

Erin laughed and Alice had a fit of giggles that wouldn't stop. She apologised to Stella with tears pouring down her face, but by now Stella was giggling too.

Erin sat down. "I'd like to go to Langsmead tomorrow," she said.

"Whatever for?" asked Alice.

"It's difficult to explain," she said, enigmatically.

Alice wasn't keen on the idea. "Do you want me to come?" she asked, hoping Erin would refuse.

"I know you've got a lot to digest, but I'd like you along if you feel up to it. I don't know when else I'll have the time. I start my new job next week."

"Oh, but I'm working tomorrow," said Stella.

"You'd have to ask Kate. There might be some function on," said Alice.

"No, there isn't," said Stella. "Ben is working down there and the hotel is closed for repairs. Two or three days I think he said."

"Right. We're on," said Erin.

Stella got up. "And I'm off to change my shift."

Erin had never been all around the whole house and Alice took both the girls on a tour. "Is this the room you talked about?" asked Stella as Alice opened the door into the green bedroom.

While they went inside Alice waited outside in the passage. That room held too many memories.

Alice showed them the door that led up to the attic rooms and went downstairs.

They were gone a while and Alice went into the kitchen. There was a box of tea on the table and as she filled up the kettle she watched Dave building a bonfire outside.

It was almost five months since Alice had last stepped into the house and although it was so familiar it felt entirely different. Perhaps it was her who was different, she reflected. So much had happened and so much had changed. Her new identity made her feel complete and there were a fresh cast of characters in her life now, including the one she waited to meet. She patted the prominent bump where her waist used to be. She was into the seventh month of her pregnancy and was told by the ante-natal clinic that the baby was doing very well. Alice was content.

She took out a mug of tea to Dave and while they chatted, Ben came by.

"Oh there you are, love," said Stella coming outside with Erin.

Stella went to give Ben a hug and Erin got out her cell phone. "I said I'd give Alex a ring when we got here," she said.

As Erin started to dial. Dave stared at her as though she was a conjurer about to perform a magic trick. At that time cell phones were not in common usage.

"You'll never get a signal here," said Ben.

"This is rural England, Erin," Alice said with a grin. "People don't use cell phones around here."

Erin grimaced and looked around. "What about that tower. I might get a reception up there."

They all glanced up at the tower dubiously. "I'll give it a try," she said. "Alex only lent me the phone so I could call him."

Alice went back into the house with her. "Do you think that doll is still here?" she asked Alice.

"I'll go and have a look if you like," said Alice.

She took out a mug of tea for Stella and Ben, but they were nowhere in sight. "He took her off into the woods," said Dave with a grin. "Right couple of love birds, them two!"

It was an effort to climb the two flights of stairs and Alice was breathless by the time she reached Poppy's former bedroom. She picked up the doll from the bed and walked off down the corridor. The door that led up to the tower was ajar and Alice hoped that Erin was all right. She called up but heard nothing. That door out to the parapet was so unwieldy and she could be trapped in there. Alice made the steep climb up the spiral staircase, huffing and puffing until she reached the top. The door opened without even a push. She stepped out onto the parapet and glanced around. There was a sudden gust of wind and the door slammed shut. She pulled on it several times but it wouldn't budge. Alice swore at the door, tried it again and finally gave it a kick.

Minutes passed and she started to panic, realising that no one would know she was there. The light had dimmed and there were dark shadows on the walls. She went over to the parapet edge and as she called out, the doll slipped out of her hand and fell over the wall. She stared down after it in dismay.

Just as she had on her first visit to the tower, Alice was overpowered by the malign atmosphere and, fuelled by fear, the moments seemed to stretch into hours. A voice cut through the ominous vacuum and she froze in terror. "No-one can hear you, not up here."

"Who is that?" said Alice, her own voice no more than a whisper.

She tried to turn around but a hand on her right shoulder restrained her. She turned to her left but another hand clamped down on her other shoulder.

Alice was now trembling. "What do you want?"

That voice came again, a woman's voice. It was deep and menacing. "I'm here to help you on your way. Think of it as a kindness."

The powerful hands pushed Alice forward and she grabbed at the wall, holding on with all her strength.

Alice flailed out with her right arm but a hand grabbed at her wrist and pulled her around so her back faced the wall.

Alice looked at her imprisoned wrist and then to the person who held it.

Stella stood facing her. "Oh my God, Alice. Are you all right?"

She slapped her hands together in front of Alice's face, so close that they almost took off her nose.

"Oh, it's you!" said Alice, letting out a sigh of relief. She glanced at Ben and Erin standing behind Stella and saw the old oak door splayed on the floor.

"Sorry, I had to do that, but you looked like you were in a trance." said Stella.

Alice nodded.

"Now take some deep breaths, will you."

Alice breathed in slowly and exhaled several times. "Someone was trying to murder me," she whispered.

"Let's get out of here," said Erin.

Once they were downstairs, Stella took charge, wrapping a blanket around Alice, checking her pulse and forcing some foul-tasting liquid into her mouth which, she discovered later, was cooking brandy Stella had discovered in the cupboard.

"I found the doll on the ground below the tower. That's how we knew where to find you," said Erin.

Stella put her arm around Alice. "And how is the patient feeling now?"

Alice stood up. "I feel okay."

She looked down anxiously at her bump. Stella ran her hand over Alice's belly and felt the baby give a kick. She smiled. "The baby's just fine. He's a right little bruiser."

"You said 'he', Stella," said Erin. "Do you think it's a boy?"

Stella laughed. "I'd put my bottom dollar on it!"

Chapter 25

Andrew glanced down the list of the people to telephone that day. He stopped at the name Alice Ainsley and back to their meeting. She had telephoned beforehand to ask whether she could see him. She didn't explain the reason for her request until she arrived at the rectory with her cousin. Andrew had only been a parish priest for three years and he had never received such an unusual petition as he did that day.

Andrew was so intrigued by the story he was told that he investigated the parish's archives for himself. There was no entry of a marriage between Eleanor Gilmore and Henry Henshaw in the marriage registry. Afterwards he turned to the baptism register and combed through the entries for the first decade of the twentieth century. That was when he came across a reference to Eleanor. She was named in the register as the mother of George Henshaw. There was another entry, two years later, that caught his eye. This one recorded the baptism of Emily, Eleanor's daughter.

"Andy, you haven't eaten your breakfast," said Lizzie. She always made Andrew a cooked breakfast on Sunday morning.

Andrew looked up at his wife as she took the baby out of the high chair. "No. I was just thinking…"

"About the sermon?"

"No, about the Henshaw case," he said, picking up his knife and fork.

"Oh?" Her baby boy was feeling heavy and Lizzie adjusted his position in her arms. "Have you talked to the Bishop yet?"

"Yes, Reggie says it's fine to go ahead," said Andrew. He looked up at her with a grin. "He could hardly say no, not after accepting that ten grand."

"Ten grand! From whom?"

"A woman in America, the granddaughter apparently."

"Good Lord! A memorial service doesn't cost that much!"

"No, it's for the church fund," he said with a smug smile. "Our Bishop is delighted!"

The headstone was made of Welsh slate and cemented into the earth beside the joint headstone where George and Emily Henshaw were buried. It was a warm, sunny day in late June and Andrew glanced in surprise at the crowd who had gathered in the church's cemetery. Word had got out and a large number of curious villagers had appeared to witness the simple memorial service.

There were many familiar faces amongst them, including Ellen Henshaw and Dave. When Alice, Erin and their party were assembled by the headstone, Andrew conducted a brief service of blessing. Afterwards, Alice and Erin stood solemnly to pay their personal respects.

Alice stared at the simple inscription, her eyes welling with tears. 'Beloved Mother of George, Emily and Lydia', it said.

"You can leave this earth now great-grandmother and be at peace. We won't forget you," she said quietly.

"Goodbye, great-grandmother. God Bless you," said Erin.

Alice gasped and clutched at Erin's hand. Erin turned to her anxiously.

"Alice?"

Alice's other hand rested on her huge stomach. She laughed. "The baby! It's starting, Erin."

"Oh, my God!" Erin exclaimed. "This boy sure knows how to pick his moment!"

Chapter 26

2008

"Are you all right, Mom?" Toby asked.

"Yes, I'm fine, darling," said Alice, smiling at her handsome young son across the table in the King's Head public house.

Toby looked dubiously at the pint of bitter in front of him. "This is warm, Mom. Shouldn't they put some ice in it?"

"No, Tobes. You wanted to try the beer from the barrel. This is how we drink it here."

The publican came up to their table with a menu and Alice looked up at him in surprise. "Ted?"

He stared at her with a frown, trying to recall her face. Ted had put on weight and his hair was now grey but his florid face was unmistakable.

Alice smiled at him. "You won't remember me because I haven't been in here for over twenty years."

"Ah, I see," he said. "Well the missus and I have been running the place for thirty years next month."

"I was a friend of Kate Tandy. She used to run the hotel, Langsmead Hall."

"Oh yes. I remember her. After they put in a new manager the hotel went downhill." He looked at her with curiosity. "So what brings you back here after all these years?"

"Sentimental reasons, Ted. I wanted to see the house again. I was in for a shock."

The Gate House beside the entrance was surprisingly unchanged and still painted in blue. Alice had turned the car left into the driveway. A tarmacked road lay ahead. She turned off the ignition and stared in confusion.

Toby had glanced at her. "What's wrong, Mom?"

"I'm afraid we're too late"

The huge cedar had gone. The house had gone. A few yards up the tarmac road stood a modern housing estate of identical red brick houses, each fronted by a neat strip of green lawn. A signpost in bold black lettering announced their arrival at 'Langsmead Close'.

"Oh, they pulled down the old place over twelve years ago. What we've got now is what they term modernity," said Ted and gave a shrug. "Still, it brings in the punters."

"Ted, please would you bring us two nice chilled lagers," said Alice.

Within minutes Ted returned and placed two glasses of lager on the table. Toby took a long drink and nodded with satisfaction. He put down his glass and looked across the table at his mother. "Mom, what happened with you and Kate? Did you see her again?" he asked.

"Yes. We met at the christening of Stella and Ben's baby."

"You mean Jess?" said Toby.

"No. Ellie."

Toby had known the family all his life and was particularly close to Jessica, the elder of the two girls. Over the years, Stella and Ben's rambling house on Wimbledon Common had become like a second home.

On their visits to England it was where Alice and the boys went to stay.

"Did you and Kate make up?"

Alice shook her head. "It was too late. By then I knew that Kate had lied to me about Julian."

It was Stella who discovered Kate's duplicity. Like Alice, Stella always read Julian's new novels when they arrived on the bookshelves and the two of them often exchanged views. One day Stella went to a book launch for his latest novel. It took place in the book department at Harrods and Julian was seated behind a table signing autographs. When Stella's turn came she introduced herself and told him she was a friend of Alice.

He stared at Stella in amazement. "Alice!" he said. Stella described how his face lit up with a smile that reached his eyes.

He asked Stella if he could talk to her later and she hung around until he was finished.

"Are you married?" she asked him in her blunt fashion. "It doesn't say a thing about your personal life on the fly leaf. Never does."

He smiled. "That's because I'm not."

"So are you still shacked up with Felicity Shaw then?"

Julian gave a puzzled frown. "Good Heavens no! Where did you get that idea? I have never co-habited with my sister-in-law. Felicity re-married years ago."

Stella said that at that point she ran out of steam. "I'm sorry," she said lamely. "I must have been misinformed."

"I don't know where that came from, but if the pundits can't dig up any dirt, they make it up," he said with a wry smile. "Let's talk about something more interesting. Tell me all about Alice."

Alice was mortified to learn of Kate's perfidiousness and determined to make immediate amends. Toby was seven years old at that time. He had known from a young age that he had a second father living in England. Julian, however, was unaware of his son's existence.

Alice agonized over the letter she sent him, expressing her regret for those lost years. She read Julian's return letter in private. There were tears streaming down her face when he said that her news had made him the happiest man on the planet.

Art was aware of Toby's paternity and later that day, when she found him alone in the den, she explained the situation. Art was a devoted husband and she would never dissemble with him. He was as sympathetic to the situation as she knew he would be and it was at his suggestion that she booked a flight to London for the first day of Toby's school vacation.

The meeting between Julian and his son took place at a restaurant in North London.

Julian had arrived early and was waiting for them at a corner table that had a good view of the entrance. His heart skipped a beat as he saw Alice enter with their young son. He stood up as they approached and gave Alice a hug. When Toby reached out his hand, he hugged him, too.

"He's just like you!" said Julian and Alice at the same moment.

They both laughed and sat down. "I chose this restaurant because I know they do good hamburgers here," said Julian with a grin.

It wasn't long before Julian and Toby were chatting like old friends and within a short period of time Julian learned a great deal about his son's life; his likes and his dislikes. He was so busy absorbing both mother and son that he hardly touched his food until Alice reminded him of it.

After the meal Julian took them over to his flat. An old-fashioned train set was laid out across the living room floor.

"I used to play with this a lot when I was your age," said Julian, looking down at the well-preserved train track with its model trains, little stations and small signal men. "I knew there must be a reason why I kept it all this time."

Throughout the following years that train set was well used. It was Toby's favourite pastime when he visited Julian. On these occasions Alice accompanied Toby to London, but she began to feel guilty about their happy reunions. Sometimes Joey came too, but in some ways that was worse. Although Art would never complain she felt it was unfair to him. He was a dedicated father to both the boys. Fatherhood was a role in which Art revelled. After Joey was born he told Alice that he wanted to be a hands-on father, not one who saw his kids only on vacations. He gave up politics and delegated most of his business affairs to a new young partner. For Alice it was a relief when Toby was old enough to travel by himself.

Toby took a drink of lager and put down the glass. "I'm sorry about earlier, Mom. I behaved like a jerk."

Alice looked across at him and smiled fondly. Toby looked so much like Julian when he was earnest. He had inherited her eyes and colouring but in most other respects he resembled his father. "Not to worry, Toby. You must have thought we were on some wild goose chase!"

"I'm sorry about the house, too. You must be disappointed," he said.

"No, darling. I'm fine about it. Langsmead Hall is imprinted on my memory. Nothing can take that away."

As they set off in the car to drive back to London, Toby turned to Alice. "Do you mind if I don't go with you tomorrow?"

"What? To visit Julian. Yes, I do mind. He'll be disappointed."

"But I promised Jess that I'd be at the barbecue."

"Oh dammit, I'd forgotten the barbecue. You'd better phone him as soon as we get back."

"But you could still go. One of us should turn up."

"No. I don't think so."

"Well, I think you should. He really wants to see you again."

Alice sat down on the bed in the room that Stella kept at her disposal. She stared at all the clothes she had pulled out of the wardrobe and thrown onto the bed. Nothing felt right for the visit she would make to Julian's flat later that morning.

As she began to re-hang the clothes in the wardrobe, she spotted a blue floral silk dress that was pushed to the end of the rail. She took it out and hoped that it would still fit. After her shower she had taken a long, hard look at herself in the bathroom mirror and didn't like what she saw. Her waist had thickened and the skin on her neck looked horribly wrinkled. She sighed. The ageing process was an inexorable fact of life. In two years' time she would be sixty years old. It was now almost a year since Art's death and during that time she hadn't taken much interest in clothes or her appearance in general, often putting on the first thing that came to hand.

Art was rarely ill and at the age of seventy-seven he appeared to be in robust health until one evening, when he and Alice returned home from a visit to friends. Art got out of the car and, as was his habit, he was on his way to open Alice's door when he collapsed on the tarmac outside their apartment block. She rushed to his side but his body was inert and she couldn't find a pulse. The doctor told her he had suffered a fatal stroke and asked whether there had been any symptoms. That evening Art had complained of a headache. Alice thought he looked pale and suggested that they leave the restaurant where they were dining. He said he had no intention of breaking up such a pleasant evening. Alice was clearly enjoying the company of their dining companions, an English couple who had recently moved to Manhattan. Afterwards people said how lucky he was to go so quickly. She heard that repeated so often that she wanted to scream in their well-meaning faces.

At the funeral chapel Alice and the boys sat with Erin, Alex and their family. She was grateful to have Stella and Ben amongst the congregation. They had flown over from England with their daughters, Jessica and Ellie. Alice was glad that the boys would have the distraction of the two pretty girls. After the formalities had been taken care of, all three families took a flight to Florida. Alice had some happy memories of that seaside home and it was a comforting place in which to grieve.

The shock of Art's sudden death had been a terrible blow. Without him there to share her life America no longer felt like home. The boys were supportive but not often around. They had their own lives to pursue. Erin saw how restless Alice was and suggested that a visit to England might do her good.

Chapter 27

Alice was nervous. She hadn't seen Julian for nine years and it would be the first time they spent time alone together since those long ago days at Langsmead. He had written to offer his condolences, but there had been no communication between them since.

The taxi dropped her off outside his flat and she walked hesitantly to the front door. Julian opened it before Alice had time to reach for the bell. He gave her a warm hug and ushered her through the doorway and into his living room. The large airy room was furnished with brown leather sofas and book-lined shelves occupied most of the wall space. Apart from the painting that hung over the mantlepiece, the room lacked any softness to offset its functional severity. The painting was of the lakeside scene.

"I'm so sorry about Art. It must have been a hellish time for you."

"Yes. It has been a bit grim. Thank you for your letter."

Alice glanced around the familiar room and nodded at the painting. "It's still there, I see. Or is it just put up when I come to visit?"

He looked at her in mock indignation. "It hasn't moved from that spot since you had it delivered to me. That must be twelve years ago now."

He poured out two glasses of champagne from the bottle in the ice bucket on the side table and handed her one.

Her hand trembled slightly as she took it from him. "What are we drinking to?"

"The future."

"Yes. To the future!" said Alice, clinking her glass against his.

She took a long sip from her glass. "I wasn't sure whether I should come. Not without Toby, I mean."

At that moment she reminded him of that vulnerable girl of over twenty years ago. "You are very lovely, Alice. Maturity sits well on you."

That infuriating flush crept up her neck. Suddenly, she felt shy. Julian's hair was now grey and there were lines on his face that she hadn't seen before, but he was still a good-looking man.

When she finished her glass of champagne, he took it from her and put down both their glasses on the table.

"Alice, I have dreamed of this moment," he said taking her hands in his. "My feelings for you haven't changed, you know. I've never stopped loving you."

Tears welled up in Alice's eyes. "And I never stopped loving you, Julian."

The End

About the author

Julia James lives in East Sussex with her three dogs and one cat. She is currently working on her second novel.

During her childhood she lived in a house called Langsmead Hall (pictured below). Like the house in the story, it was later demolished to make way for a modern housing estate.